Alaska—the last frontier.

The nights are long. The days are cold.

*And the men are really, really **HOT!***

*Can you think of a better excuse
for a trip up north?*

*Come on back to the unorthodox
and unforgettable town of Good Riddance
and experience some*

ALASKAN HEAT

The nights don't get any longer than this...

Dear Reader,

Welcome back, yet again, to Good Riddance, Alaska, where the citizens and visitors get to "leave behind what ails them." But sometimes life isn't so much about leaving things behind as it is dealing with those things you've avoided the most. And that's precisely the situation facing my hero and heroine—the handsome, footloose and fancy-free Sven Sorenson and Good Riddance's quietly intense bush pilot, Juliette Miller.

Both Sven and Juliette have to dig deep to find out exactly what they're made of before they can figure out that they're made for each other. People come with a myriad of problems, some of which run deeper than others. And while we're not responsible for another human being, we can offer love and support and acceptance. Sometimes, as Sven and Juliette discover, love enables us to see the best in someone. And that insight buoys them up to be the person we know they can be.

I hope you enjoy watching Sven and Juliette discover a lot about themselves...and each other.

If you did, please let me know. I love to hear from my readers. Visit me at www.jenniferlabrecque.com.

And as always...happy reading!

Jen

Jennifer LaBrecque

NORTHERN FIRES

™ Harlequin®

TORONTO NEW YORK LONDON
AMSTERDAM PARIS SYDNEY HAMBURG
STOCKHOLM ATHENS TOKYO MILAN MADRID
PRAGUE WARSAW BUDAPEST AUCKLAND

Recycling programs
for this product may
not exist in your area.

ISBN-13: 978-0-373-79687-8

NORTHERN FIRES

This edition published by arrangement with Harlequin Books S.A.

For questions and comments about the quality of this book please contact us at Customer_eCare@Harlequin.ca.

® and TM are trademarks of the publisher. Trademarks indicated with ® are registered in the United States Patent and Trademark Office, the Canadian Trade Marks Office and in other countries.

www.Harlequin.com

Printed in U.S.A.

ABOUT THE AUTHOR

After a varied career path that included barbecue-joint waitress, corporate number-cruncher and bug-business maven, Jennifer LaBrecque has found her true calling writing contemporary romance. Named 2001 Notable New Author of the Year and 2002 winner of the prestigious Maggie Award for Excellence, she is also a two-time RITA® Award finalist. Jennifer lives in suburban Atlanta with a Chihuahua who runs the whole show.

Books by Jennifer LaBrecque

To get the inside scoop on Harlequin Blaze and its talented writers, be sure to check out blazeauthors.com.

All backlist available in ebook. Don't miss any of our special offers. Write to us at the following address for information on our newest releases.

Harlequin Reader Service
U.S.: 3010 Walden Ave., P.O. Box 1325, Buffalo, NY 14269
Canadian: P.O. Box 609, Fort Erie, Ont. L2A 5X3

To Susan Kimoto Floyd and Lucius Williams, IV.
Thank you.

1

"HEY, HOTTIE, wait up, I've been looking for you."

Sven Sorenson, heading down the only real street in Good Riddance, Alaska, stopped.

He'd recognize that voice anywhere. Grinning, he turned. "How's my favorite girl?"

Alberta Reynolds, her bright red hair sticking out sporadically from a yellow-and-purple scarf rather like a hedgehog, returned his grin, minus a few teeth here and there. Her bottom lip bulged with the dip of smokeless tobacco she kept tucked there.

Alberta was something of a living legend in these parts. She claimed descent from European Gypsy stock, psychic powers and unparalleled matchmaking abilities. Sven had always been a skeptic when it came to that psychic stuff and he figured people either clicked or they didn't, but Alberta had a reputation for putting together lasting hookups. Well, except for when it came to herself. Already married five times, rumor had it Alberta was on the lookout for Husband Number Six.

She'd shown up yesterday, her beat-up Datsun pickup—the hood held on with baling wire—pulling a one-room travel trailer that appeared damn near as old as Alberta herself, and that was pretty old. A couple of years ago she'd adopted a three-legged cat she'd named Lord Byron.

Sven and Alberta had crossed paths numerous times in the past ten years in the small towns scattered across Alaska's vast wilderness. Sven in his capacity as a professional builder, Alberta in her capacity as a Gypsy queen. She was a hoot for sure and had a good heart.

"I heard you were here," she said.

He gave her a quick hug. "Are you following me again?" he said with a smile as he released her.

It was a running joke between them. Sven was almost as much of a rolling stone as Alberta. He'd followed work all over the state for years, preferring the smaller towns to Anchorage's sprawl.

"You know it. Heard you've been here nearly ten months. That's some kind of record for you."

He shrugged. "I was lucky enough to win the contract to build the new day spa, then it burned. I had remodel work in the winter and then rebuilding the spa, and Skye and Dalton's place. Now I'm knee-deep in a new build and a remodel project. I like it here, so it's all good."

For the first time he'd had an odd reluctance to leave a place. Well, actually, *this* place. He'd done a couple of jobs over the years in Good Riddance. Packing up and changing locations had never been a problem before. And it wasn't that it was a exactly a *problem* now, he'd just been glad to stay put for a while.

He pushed aside the thought and picked back up on the banter. "You've got to quit chasing me this way, Alberta. People are going to talk."

"Always." She winked at him. "I know a good catch when I see one."

Which was questionable considering her five matrimonial forays. Sven supposed the flip side of that was five times she'd snagged what had seemed a good catch at the time.

Sven nodded in the direction of her travel trailer. "I was going to stop by yesterday, but your truck was gone. I waved at Lord Byron though." The big orange-and-yellow tomcat had been sitting in the window, basking in the sun.

She nodded. "I had a house call to make."

Alberta's matchmaking service involved house calls, where she'd actually show up at the cabins of some of the more remote bachelors in these parts.

"Who are you hooking up this time?"

"Dwight Simmons."

"Dwight?" Not much surprised Sven, but that caught his attention.

Dwight was eighty if he was a day. For years he and Jeb Taylor had been near-permanent fixtures in the Good Riddance airstrip office where they argued and played a slow-moving game of chess. Jeb had died last summer and now Dwight mostly sat there lost.

"You're never too old for love…and he's lonely." She slanted him an arch glance from beneath her painted-on eyebrows. "I'd say you're ready for love, too. I think you're lonely, Sven."

She was smiling, but there was a glint in her eyes, a knowing, as if she really could see somewhere deep inside him. It was a little freaky. Damn. Goose bumps popped up on him that had nothing to do with the weather. Actually it was a lot freaky.

In all their years of crossing paths, Alberta had never tried her hocus-pocus on Sven. And now she was as wrong as the day was long in July.

"Do I look lonely?"

A beat-to-hell-and-back Suburban drove by. Petey, the prospector who doubled as the resident taxi service, honked and waved. Alberta and Sven waved back.

Alberta focused on Sven, eyeing him consideringly. Despite his prickle of discomfort at her eyeballing him, he crossed his arms over his chest and laughed. Alberta was a trip.

"You look *ready*."

"Ready for…" This was getting better and better. He was amused and curious as to what she was going to come up with next.

"You're ready for a meaningful relationship, a commitment."

Okay, so maybe he had thought now and again that it would be nice to have someone to come home to at night and maybe have a couple of kids, but he'd never admit it to Alberta.

Grinning, he shook his head. "Alberta, you are way off the mark."

Her wide smile called him a liar. "No way, hottie. I'm never wrong about these things. You're ready to find a woman to come home to and snuggle up with every night. Weren't you just thinking at your father's birthday celebration that you want what your brother has?"

Her words zapped a shiver of acknowledgment down his spine and wiped the grin off his face. How the hell could she know…? A month ago he'd gone back to Wasilla for his pop's sixtieth birthday. Sven's brother, Eric, Eric's wife and their five-month-old daughter had been there, as well. Watching them interact had given him the funniest feeling inside, and yes, he had thought exactly that—he wanted what they had.

An image of darkly sexy Juliette Miller, one of

Good Riddance's bush pilots, had popped into his mind. He'd quickly dismissed Juliette and the notion.

He zeroed in on the one detail Alberta had gotten wrong. "I'm not a snuggler."

Her expression was nothing short of smug. "You will be."

Another shiver chased from his neck down his back. "I'm not one of your matchmaking candidates."

"Oh, but you are. The problem is sometimes you men don't know your own mind." Damn if that wasn't the same thing his mother and his sister-in-law said sometimes. *Women.*

"My mind and I communicate just fine." Sven laughed. "There's no business to be had on my end." He so did not need a matchmaker. He did just fine with chicks on his own.

"For you, my services are free." A sly smile lit her eyes and curled her lips. "And here comes the one for you."

Sven turned. The small hairs on the back of his neck stood at attention. Across the street Juliette, her short dark hair hugging her head, a pair of aviator glasses hiding her eyes, was striding down the sidewalk. As usual, purposeful intent marked her every step. She was standoffish as hell. They'd managed to give each other a wide berth, which was kind of strange considering they were singles of the opposite sex. However, when a woman steadfastly ignored you, ignoring her in return became something of a game. It'd require a brave man or a fool to take on Juliette. He was neither.

He turned back around and faced Alberta. "I've got some sad news for you, Alberta. You've got this one wrong. I like my women uncomplicated and easy."

Eyes gleaming, Alberta shot him a pitying look. "And look at where it's gotten you." She patted his arm. "You'll see."

Right. More like Alberta would see, because not just no, but hell no. Juliette Miller required way too much work.

"It's broken." Dr. Skye Shanahan pointed to the X-ray film up on the backlit screen that afforded a clear view of Bull's left arm.

"Well, dammit, if that's not inconvenient," Bull grumbled from where he sat on the exam table.

"Inconvenient's a whole lot better than dead," said Good Riddance's founder, town mayor, but most important, Bull's wife, Merrilee Danville Weatherspoon Swenson. She was glad he wasn't dead—and now she just might kill him for taking such a stupid risk. Climbing up on top of the roof to string Christmas lights in May....

"Now I've got to turn the set building over to someone else," Bull said.

Merrilee simply shook her head. Honest to goodness, forget the pain of a broken bone, the man was upset because ever since they'd started the annual spring dinner theater six years ago, Bull had handled the set design. That was one of the things that had set her head over heels in love with him when she first met him twenty-five years ago: he was one interesting mix of a man. Tough as nails, he uncompromisingly adhered to a fitness schedule, bore a plethora of physical and emotional scars compliments of a stint at the Hanoi Hilton during the Vietnam War, wore his long gray hair pulled back in a ponytail, and had the talent and soul of an artist even though he ran a hardware store. At this moment, disappointment etched his face.

Granted, the dinner theater production was a big deal. It was one of those things that involved everyone. If people didn't want to be part of the production, they could just sit in the audience. They'd all chosen to live in an area where entertainment was scarce, but forming a dinner theater had built on their strong sense of community and brought a creative outlet to lots of folks who didn't have one otherwise.

"Sven," Merrilee said. The tall blond builder wasn't exactly a Good Riddance resident—yet—but he was the logical choice to take over for Bull. Plus, there was the Juliette issue.

"Well, he knows how to build," Bull admitted, "but it takes some artistry, as well."

"I'm sure he won't be as good as you, but he does have something of an artistic bent, as well," Merrilee said, understating Sven's capabilities so as not to trample all over her husband's already-bruised ego.

"You don't say."

From the khaki-green walls of the exam room, a giant yellow smiley face painted on the opposite wall beamed at them, in stark contrast to Bull's hangdog expression.

Merrilee rubbed her hand over his flannel-clad arm—the unbroken one. "Just for this season, sweetie."

"All right then. I guess you better go look into it before everyone's freaking out that I won't be handling it. You don't need to stay while Dr. Skye puts on the cast. You know, Sven might not be able to handle all that comes with the job, if you know what I mean. Juliette has definite ideas about what she does and doesn't want."

It had taken some prodding and more than a little wheedling for Merrilee to rope Juliette into working on the set design with Bull this year. Juliette was pleasant enough, but she totally kept to herself. However, once Merrilee had dropped by the cabin outside of town Juliette rented and had seen all the wind chimes Juliette created, she knew the theater production was the perfect way to involve Juliette in the community. Juliette, still reserved for the most part, had taken to it like a fish to water.

"Juliette is doing a great job, isn't she?"

Merrilee loved being right. Thank goodness she was most of the time, because when she was wrong…well, she did wrong in a big way. Plus, she'd thought for the longest time that Juliette might be just what Sven needed, but she'd had enough God-given sense to keep her mouth shut on that one. It was going to be ding-dang hard for Sven and Juliette to steadfastly ignore one another the way they had for the past ten months if they were working together on the set. *Hmm.* Merrilee wasn't glad Bull had broken his arm, but most of the time things happened for a reason.

"Who knows? He might not even want to. If he doesn't, we'll figure something out."

Merrilee didn't want to further agitate her normally unflappable husband, so she held her own counsel. But she was ninety-nine percent sure Sven would be thrilled to be part of the production.

Propping against the door frame of the Good Riddance Community Center, her clipboard tucked under one arm, Juliette worried her lower lip with her teeth. She'd heard from half a dozen people as they'd filtered in that Bull had broken his arm—news traveled at warp speed in a town of less than a thousand. He was going to be fine, but now they were in a pickle with the set. She'd better come up with an alternative and fast.

The air hummed with excitement as a group practiced their lines onstage. Off to the right, Ellie Lightfoot worked on altering a costume. In just a couple of months she would become Ellie Sisnukett when she and Nelson married. They were both quiet, but the town would miss them when they left for Nelson to go to med school.

From the lighting area, Tessa Sisnukett, the director, tested the spots and backlighting since the lighting guy, her husband, Clint, was on a guide trip. The sharp squeals of a group of kids playing a game of tag in the back of the room added to the mix.

Alberta, the Gypsy queen, had shown up two days ago and appointed herself the play's special consultant, as they were performing a romantic comedy and Alberta specialized in affairs of the heart. Juliette hadn't had any direct dealings with her, but she was slightly in awe of Alberta, whose reputation preceded her. Juliette had thought for one crazy minute about maybe asking for a "reading," but had dismissed the idea just as quickly. Her life was finally on something of an even keel. If her future held a big nosedive, it was probably best to not know.

Alberta was plopped in a folding chair opposite Norris Watts who'd started up a monthly newspaper for Good Riddance and the surrounding area. Norris had approached Juliette about doing a feature article on her as a female bush pilot. Juliette had been

nice, but firm, in turning her down. She didn't want to think about her past, her ex-husbands or her parents, and inevitably a feature article would mean that kind of digging.

She'd finally learned to live in the moment and that's exactly where she wanted to stay and what she wanted to focus on.

Even though it was pushing seven in the evening, daylight still filtered through the windows, turning Alberta's red hair into a torch atop her head. Juliette wasn't sure if she'd ever get used to the 2:00 a.m. sunrise and 10:00 p.m. sunsets that came with the territory. However, she wasn't complaining. Spring and summer's long days of sunlight were a welcome change from winter's cold dark. Growing up in North Carolina, Juliette had always welcomed the change of seasons but never as much as now that she lived in Alaska.

And daylight or not, what was she going to do about finishing up the backdrop for the second scene?

The door opened and Merrilee slipped into the room, a coffee cup in her hand.

"Just the woman I wanted to see," Merrilee said, closing the door behind her. "I'm sure you heard about Bull."

Juliette nodded. "He's okay?"

"He'll be fine, just bummed that he can't finish

the set. But I wanted to let you know I've talked to Sven and he's more than willing to pitch in."

"Sven Sorenson?" Juliette tensed, her stomach feeling all wonky. She felt wonky every time she caught sight of Sven.

Merrilee laughed. "As far as I know he's the only Sven in town."

"But…" Juliette trailed off because there really wasn't any rational reason why Sven couldn't take over building the set design.

Merrilee peered at her over the rim of her raised cup, her blue eyes gleaming in amusement. Merrilee ran the Good Riddance B & B and the airstrip that had become Juliette's base station. Of course, as founder and mayor, Merrilee also ran the town. Merrilee's still-prominent Southern accent and her way of taking charge without being abrasive so reminded Juliette of the good bits and pieces, few as there were, of her childhood in North Carolina.

Even though she kept a distance, Juliette identified with Merrilee. Merrilee, caught up in a situation not to her liking in her first marriage, had loaded up a camper and drove until she'd found a place that brought her peace and a measure of solace—a reprieve from the life she no longer found acceptable. She'd parked her motor home and founded the town of Good Riddance.

It wasn't exactly Juliette's story, but Juliette could relate to being in a bad situation where she'd been the only one who could save herself. She, too, had found refuge and some measure of peace in Alaska and the skies above this vast land. She'd wanted a fresh start and when she'd heard about the bush pilot position in Good Riddance and then the town slogan, "Welcome to Good Riddance, where you leave behind what ails you," it seemed the perfect place for her. And it seemed she had indeed left behind a legacy of two alcoholic parents and then her own history with alcohol. She'd been here two years and mercifully, chaos had not followed her. While her aloneness was occasionally lonely, it was also peaceful, and there was a whole lot to be said for that.

And not much—as in nothing—escaped Merrilee's shrewd assessment, just as now when Juliette was hemming and hawing and hedging.

"But what? Bull can't handle the set design with his broken arm, and with Sven being right here and artistic, to boot, it just makes sense. To tell you the truth, I think Sven wanted to work on it but didn't want to step on Bull's toes, since Bull has always handled the job. What is it that you don't like about Sven?"

"It's not that I don't like him…"

Merrilee leveled another all-seeing glance Juliette's way. Juliette shifted from one foot to another. "It's not that I dislike him, he just makes me, well, I guess a little uncomfortable."

"How's that?"

If she said that there was something faintly dangerous about him—not sinister, but dangerous—she'd sound like a nut. And she didn't find him physically dangerous—it was more that she intuitively knew that he could be dangerous to her emotionally. She found him unsettling. "He's too..." Once again she stumbled, not sure what she wanted to say.

"Good-looking? Funny? Charming? Outgoing? Flirtatious?"

Yes, yes and yes. She was altogether too aware of how conscious she was of him on all levels whenever he was in proximity. Therefore, she had pointedly avoided said proximity as the safest route. "Well, there is all of that."

"He's a nice guy, Juliette. He knows his way around power tools. He's a craftsman and an artist—"

"He's an artist?" She'd always thought of artists as kind of dark and brooding...or gay. Sven was none of the above.

"After a fashion. There's definitely artistry in his work and he does some sketching as a hobby."

"Sketching?" Despite herself, she was intrigued. "I had no idea."

Merrilee smiled. "It's not something he's likely to talk about over a brew at Gus's. Likewise, he probably has no idea you make wind chimes."

It wasn't something she went around blabbing about. She'd always loved how expressive wind chimes were. The ones Juliette made weren't always harmonious, but then again, they reflected life as she knew it.

Alberta and Norris, their business apparently concluded, wandered over. "How's Bull?" Norris asked.

"Grumpy. He's a terrible patient."

"Show me a man who isn't," Alberta said. "And I should know. Although come to think of it, my fourth husband wasn't that much of a whiner when he was sick, but Lester, number five, that man would moan over a hangnail."

Now, there was a woman not afraid to give matrimony a chance—over and over again. Five husbands. Wow. Two had been plenty for Juliette...and then some. Both of them had been big mistakes and she'd learned her lesson. In her book, three strikes meant you were out and she had no intention of going back to bat in that particular game.

They all laughed in the way of women amused over the foibles of men. "Well, at least Bull's not a whiner," Merrilee said. "I'll take gruff over whineage any day, but I can only take so much. He's not much of a patient and I'm not much of a nurse." Merrilee shared a conspiratorial smile. "Why do you think I'm here instead of there?"

Norris snorted.

"Actually, I was just telling Juliette that Sven's going to take over the set work."

Alberta nodded. "Good choice."

"Easy on the eyes, too," Norris said in her smoke-graveled voice.

"We were just discussing that," Merrilee said.

Good God almighty, the last thing Juliette wanted was for Norris and Alberta to think she was losing her mind over Sven's blond good looks. So, maybe she did avoid him because there was this sort of tingle that started whenever he was around. Maybe he was drop-dead gorgeous in a rugged kind of way. Maybe she had once had a dream where he was a Viking marauder and she'd been willingly plundered. Maybe all that was true, but she didn't plan to breathe a word of that to anyone because it simply didn't matter. "We were discussing that he's a good choice, not the easy-on-the-eyes part."

"I thought we covered the easy-on-the-eyes part, too," Merrilee said, obviously teasing.

Alberta looked at Juliette. "Sven and I go back a long way. He's good people. I think you'll like what he can do with his hands and his imagination."

Juliette had plenty of her own imagination and it zoomed from zero to sixty as to just what those hands would feel like trailing against her skin, sifting through her hair, stroking against parts that hadn't been stroked by anyone other than her in a long time. Juliette redirected her wayward thoughts. Plywood. Fabric. Paint. That's what Alberta meant.

This was what made Sven Sorenson dangerous. The man wasn't even in the room and simply the thought of him set her pulse racing. How on earth was she going to work with him?

"He has to check on some things over at the spa, but he said he'll drop by afterward so you can bring him up to speed. Does that work for you?"

There was nothing left to say, no protest to mount without looking like a total idiot. "Sure. No problem."

She could focus and tingle all at the same time, couldn't she?

2

SVEN DROPPED IN THE last hinge pin on the supply door. He glanced over his shoulder when he heard Jenna behind him.

"Oh, yeah, that looks better," she said. "Thanks so much." She threw arms wide as if encompassing her entire space, her smile as big as her embrace. Neither was, however, as big as her very pregnant belly. Sven made a concerted effort to keep his mouth from gaping open. Jenna's tummy was bigger than her chest these days and that was saying something... actually, that was saying a lot. He hadn't spent much time around pregnant women. He'd kind of wondered if his sister-in-law might explode before her due date. Jenna was in the same boat. "Aren't you just loving it?" she said.

He nodded. "It's awesome." Sven had built Jenna Rathburne Jeffries's new day-spa facility and her living quarters upstairs. Actually, he'd built it twice. The first time around it had burned down when there was a fluke problem with a junction box. They'd had to wait on the spring thaw to rebuild it.

It was Jenna's first home and it had turned out great. The spa on the ground floor and the living space above imparted a sense of tranquility, with large windows offering views of the evergreens, distant mountains and the sky. A built-in waterfall in the reception area lent the sound of running water throughout the ground floor. Speakers piped the original recordings of a Native musician throughout the rooms. It was soothing and elegant without being pretentious. He was just knocking out the final punch list while his crew worked on their new primary project, a huge house a couple of miles out of town for a mysterious new owner. All the plans had been via an attorney, fax and secondary email.

Jenna's cat, Tama, bumped against Sven's legs. Sven leaned down and ran his hand over the cat's thick fur. "Hey, big guy."

Jenna had been a dream to work with. Actually, Jenna was pretty much a man's dream in and of herself—blonde, curvy in all the right places, fun, easygoing and outgoing. Just about every man within a five-hundred-mile radius had been despondent when she'd married Logan Jeffries. Sven, however, hadn't been despondent. He'd been more along the lines of confounded with himself. Jenna was exactly the kind of woman he'd always been attracted to. He and she had even sort of given it a try. Early on they'd kissed. While he liked her and she liked him, there'd been absolutely nothing close to a spark.

No, instead, he had to be plagued with some crazy-ass attraction to Juliette Miller, which he'd done his damnedest to deny, considering she had *complicated* written all over her and had never given him the time of day.

"So, you're taking over the set design for the play?"

Sven wasn't remotely surprised Jenna already knew. He didn't even question how. News spread faster in Good Riddance than the clap in a low-rent whorehouse.

"Yeah. I'm heading over to meet with Juliette as soon as I finish up here."

"You'll love her."

What the hell? First Alberta with her off-the-wall prognostications and now Jenna. "I'm just going to finish up the set and it's not as if I don't know her from around town."

Jenna peered at him as if he'd lost his mind. "I know. I did the hair and makeup last year and I'm doing it again this year." She patted her enormous belly. "Well, maybe. Some people can't tell you what they want, but Juliette can. She and I were talking the other day about the play, which makes it so much easier. That's what I mean—you'll love working with her." Comprehension dawned. "Oh...you thought I meant you'd *love* her. Well, you could be onto something there." She tilted her head to one side, nodding. "You're right. The two of you would make a cute couple."

"I'm not onto anything and I didn't say we'd make a cute couple."

"But you would."

"She's not my type."

"Well, what's your type?"

"You." Although he suspected Jenna's waters ran a little deeper than he'd first thought, he liked his women like a clear mountain stream, and Juliette was more like a dark, still lake and who knew what was going to be beneath that surface.

Jenna laughed unselfconsciously. "Yeah, well, we see where that got both of us." She rubbed her tummy again. He wished she'd quit doing that—he had nothing to do with her present state of impending motherhood, but Jenna was known for switching more than just a few train tracks in a conversation. "You might've thought I was your type, but I wasn't really your type. So, it's this mistaken notion of what your type is that's got you still single now."

Did all women study the same sound track to throw back at men?

"I like being single." Not the whole-truth-and-nothing-but-the-truth, but he was feeling cornered by crazy female talk.

"Then why are you talking about falling in love with Juliette?"

The mere notion gave him a funny feeling in the pit of his gut. But then again, it would probably affect any guy that way. God help him. If it was anyone other than Jenna, who he knew tended to talk in circles.… "I'm not. You are."

"You are too because you're talking to me and that's what we're talking about."

He gave up. "I'm just going to work on the set. Nothing more. Nothing less. I don't even know her."

"Do any of us really know one another until we've put in a little effort? And tell me you're not curious about her. But then again, I doubt you're her type."

"What the hell does that mean?"

"Well, I think Juliette's pretty particular, because in the year and a half I've lived here I've never known her to date anyone. For that matter, I've never seen her at any of the karaoke nights or the exercise classes at the community center. She's nice and she's not unfriendly, but she keeps to herself."

"Okay. But how does that mean I'm not her type?"

Jenna shrugged. "I dunno. She just strikes me as kind of serious—"

That struck a nerve. Just because he was easygoing it didn't necessarily mean he was a lightweight. "I can be serious."

"Wow, okay. I didn't mean anything by it. I'm sure you can."

"But what? There's a *but* there."

"Well, don't take this the wrong way—" that never boded good things to come "—but she really hasn't shown the slightest bit of interest in you that I've ever noticed, so, you know…"

He wasn't an egomaniac but damn, a man was entitled to a little pride and Jenna had just crushed his beneath her heel by pointing out the obvious. Juliette had never given him the proverbial time of day.

"Thanks, Jenna."

"Oh, Sven, I didn't mean to hurt your feelings. I guess I just didn't realize you felt that way about Juliette."

"I don't feel any way about her." Which wasn't exactly true, but this wasn't a soul-baring session with a shrink, either, was it? He had to admit his masculine pride had been pricked from the get-go because Juliette had taken one look at him and dismissed him. WTF was up with that? He'd decided then and there she'd be too complicated and too much trouble.

"Well, maybe you should test the waters, the way you and I did, so you'll know. It's impossible for a good-looking single guy to be ambivalent about a pretty woman of similar age in a town this size. You do think she's pretty, don't you? And she has a nice figure."

"Of course she's pretty." There was something arresting about her short dark hair, brown eyes and delicately sculpted face. "And yes, she has a nice figure." Yes, he had noticed her soft curves on more than one occasion—well, the truth of the matter was, every time he saw her. "And as you so graciously pointed out, darling, she's never given me the time of day."

"Maybe she's as scared of you as you are of her."

"Wait a minute. I didn't say I was scared of her."

"You didn't have to. You think she's a babe, but you've never asked her out so that can only mean one thing. You're scared." She patted him on the back. "Don't be. What's the worst she can say? No."

"I am not scared."

"Good. Let me know what she says."

"About what?"

"When you ask her out."

Juliette made a couple of notes, but her concentration was seriously compromised waiting on Sven to show up. She was ridiculously nervous. He was going to go over the set design with her. Big deal. She'd seen him around town any number of times in the past ten months. Therefore, it was totally silly and uncalled for that she'd popped into the ladies' room twice now to check her hair and make sure she didn't have any mascara smudges beneath her eyes.

She heard the pull of a diesel truck passing outside, but it didn't stop. She moved to the center front, looking at the now-empty stage. The rest of the cast and crew had vaporized as if they'd been caught up in a Vulcan mind meld. Instead, it had simply been the allure of Thursday-night karaoke over at Gus's. Good Riddance citizens took their karaoke seriously.

While Juliette stopped in at Gus's for meals, she didn't make a habit of hanging out there. Most days she felt good and strong, but spending a lot of extra time in a bar didn't seem the wisest course of action. Once an alcoholic always an alcoholic. A recovered drunk was only one drink away from being back at it… And she never wanted to be back at it again.

She was a big girl. She could handle being alone with Sven Sorenson. She was alone with men all the time, flying them in and out of Good Riddance and to various and sundry spots in remote Alaska. He was just another man. Granted, he had a larger-than-life quality about him that wasn't just because of his height. As Merrilee had pointed out earlier, Sven was just too…too everything—handsome, charming, sexy, she could throw in another sexy just to keep it real and accurate—for a woman's peace of mind. And since Juliette was all about preserving the peace—primarily her own—she'd gone out of her way to keep her distance from Sven Sorenson.

She smiled ruefully to herself. The community center was far larger than the confines of her airplane. Distance shouldn't be a problem.

Despite her newfound perspective, her heart began to thud in her chest at the unmistakable sound of a diesel truck pulling into the parking lot outside.

The engine died, followed by the slam of a door and the crunch of boots on gravel.

She pasted on her most professional smile—friendly, yet distant—as boots thudded on the wood stairs and hesitated at the door. The door opened and Sven stood there for a moment. Perhaps she was simply in dramatic mode, courtesy of rehearsal, but it was like some frame in a movie where the gorgeous hero pauses so all the females in the audience can indulge in a swoonfest.

She was an audience of one, but certainly not immune to the visual picture he presented. His booted feet planted apart, strong, long legs in worn denim, narrow hips, a broad chest and still-broader shoulders. The spring sunlight served as a backlight, burnishing his hair to molten gold. He was a cross between a Viking marauder and a Norse god.

All the spit dried right out of her mouth and seemed to head south to congregate between her thighs in a totally unexpected, unwelcome flood of physical attraction.

It was like being struck by a bolt of lightning—not that she ever had been but this must be what it felt like. Of course, she'd noticed him before. He was an extremely good-looking man. A woman would have to be dead not to notice a tall, broad-shouldered, muscled man with a well-chiseled face, blond hair, dark blue eyes that sometimes took on a hint of moss green, a ready smile and an outgoing personality. So she had been aware of him, but never, ever like this. This total rush of energy, attraction, awareness—whatever label she wanted to throw on it—was exhilarating…and terrifying.

She realized while she was in some kind of freak-ish sexual stupor, he was simply allowing his eyes to adjust to the room. "Juliette?"

She'd been gawking and he hadn't even seen her, thank goodness. She gathered her wits, along with her notes, and stepped forward. "Right here. Hi."

He stepped inside and closed the door behind him. "Hi." He smiled and Juliette curled her fingers tighter around her clipboard. "I hear you've got some set-design work that needs finishing up," he said. "I'm your man…I…uh…if you want me." He shifted. "Well, you know what I mean…for the play."

Juliette was flummoxed…and she didn't flummox easily. "i…uh…sure. I hate that Bull can't do it, but I appreciate you offering to help."

"Sure thing." From the first time she'd heard him speak, his voice had always reminded her of her aunt Mae's apple pie, which had always been her favorite dessert—crisp notes with an underlying hint of honey and spice. "You want to bring me up to speed with where you are and what you need?"

Where she was and what she needed…well, she could write a short story on both of those with a footnote on what she might actually want on a temporary basis. However, Sven hadn't meant it in the personal sense, which she would've never shared with him anyway.

"Let me give you a quick rundown on the play and then I'll show you what we have so far."

He straddled a chair and turned those midnight-blue eyes on her. She sat in a chair a few feet away, her pulse still not quite back in the at-ease range she usually aimed to maintain.

She gave him the CliffsNotes version of the storyline. Interestingly, she could almost see the wheels turning in his head, fitting in the backdrop and set design to the plot and its various segments. Juliette wrapped it up and said as she stood, "And this is what we have so far."

He rose to his feet, as well. She was very much aware of his height and the impressive breadth of his chest and shoulders. And yeah, that was all good and fine, but what could he do with the set?

Silently she turned on her heel and he followed as she led him to the back right corner behind the curtained stage where Bull had set up his work area. Sven's boots echoed across the stage floor as he walked with her. Shadows shrouded Bull's section behind the drop of the heavy curtain. An element of awareness threaded the silence between them.

In the dim light, Juliette inhaled Sven's scent—a combination of man, fresh-cut lumber, soap, leather and the outdoors. Her heart raced as he leaned in and reached toward her—her thoughts racing nearly as fast as her heart.

It had been so long since she'd been kissed or touched by a man...well, by anyone for that matter. Did she want to feel his palm against her skin? Did she want the sensation of his breath mingling with hers? Did she want to know the taste of his lips and tongue against her own?

She wasn't sure.

She stood as if frozen and everything seemed to move in extreme slow motion as he drew even with her. His arm brushed against her shoulder, setting off a series of tremors inside her.

There was a sudden movement, a click and light flooded the area. He dropped his arm to his side.

"That sheds a little light on it, doesn't it?" he said.

Oh, God, she was losing her mind. She'd thought he was going to kiss her and all he was doing was turning on the freaking light. And the worst of it was, she was disappointed. What was wrong with her?

"Thanks," she said, taking a step away from him. "That definitely makes it easier to see."

Sven crossed his big arms over his chest and tucked his chin down, studying the pieces before them. Finally he nodded. "It works."

She was relieved. She and Bull had always been in sync. She hadn't been too sure that Sven would get what she wanted, but apparently he did. "I think it does. I do think this is a little off, but I can't put my finger on the exact problem."

He cocked his head to one side, assessing the plywood cutout. Finally he looked from the piece to her. "If we smooth out this line a bit—" he traced the line with his finger in the air "—and make that one sharper..."

She could see it in her mind's eye. Juliette nodded. "Perfect, that would take care of the problem." She found it somewhat surprising that they seemed to be on the same wavelength.

"I have a couple of other ideas that might work, too." He paused. "Have you had dinner yet?"

She often didn't eat until late in the evening at this time of year. She found she followed a different rhythm with the longer days of sunlight. "No. I had a busy flight schedule today and then rehearsal." She liked sitting in on the rehearsal and seeing if what they had on the set side was working or not.

He grinned, and she found breathing a bit more difficult. "And then you had to wait on me to come by. Sorry to hold you up. Jenna had a couple of kinks that needed smoothing out over at the spa."

"No problem. I just appreciate your help with the set, and so does everyone else involved with the production." She tacked on that last bit just to make sure he knew she wasn't being personal when she thanked him and that he didn't think she had any kind of agenda. Because she didn't. Nope. None.

"I'd say let's drop by Gus's but it's karaoke night. It'd be pretty difficult to talk there."

She smiled. "Impossible is more like it."

"I left a roast going in the Crock-Pot. Definitely nothing fancy, but it usually turns out good enough. Want to come over and have a bite to eat and we can knock around some ideas?"

Juliette made it a practice to keep to herself. It just seemed easier that way. So, normally she would've thanked him politely and declined. However, normal seemed to have checked out on vacation, because instead of declining she found herself saying, "I could do that."

"You know, I'm out at Shadow Lake."

Juliette smiled. "Right."

Shadow Lake was beyond lovely. The large tract of property wasn't too far out of town. At the heart sat a lake that got its name from the mountains surrounding it—at almost any time of day different parts of the lake were shadowed by one mountain or another.

It had belonged to two sisters who had retired to Good Riddance to raise sled dogs and enjoy the Alaskan lifestyle. Irene and Erlene Marbut had become part of Good Riddance's lore. While the sisters didn't want to live together, neither had they wanted to live too far apart, so they'd built cabins within spitting distance on the edge of Shadow Lake.

The two women, now deceased, had willed their

property to Dalton Saunders, Juliette's fellow bush pilot. Last year Dalton had married Skye Shanahan, who had taken over as the local doctor following her stint as a relief doc. The couple had contracted Sven to build them a new home that was a bit more private and offered room for them to start a family.

Juliette had heard Sven was staying in one of the original cabins while he renovated the other, and then he'd switch until they were both done. The two side-by-side cabins would be for visiting family members. Skye's snooty family had actually fallen in love with both Alaska and their outspoken, slightly outrageous son-in-law.

"Well, of course you know, since you fly with Dalton. Plus, there doesn't seem to be much that people in Good Riddance don't know about each other."

"True enough." Although there was plenty about Juliette that wasn't known—and she planned to keep it that way. Some things were better left unsaid and in the past.

3

SVEN GLANCED IN HIS REARVIEW mirror to confirm Juliette was behind him as he hung a right onto the unpaved road to the cabins. The road, spread with a fresh load of crusher-run gravel, cut through the stately spruce trees. He looked back to the driveway just in time to brake and stop.

Juliette halted behind him. He stuck his head out the window and yelled back to her, "Beaver crossing the road."

She flashed a smile and nodded, giving him the thumbs-up. Her smile sent heat through him.

Bucky, as Sven had dubbed the beaver, stopped midcrossing and looked at him. Sven waited. Unperturbed he'd interrupted traffic, Bucky once again continued his journey. Sven had sighted a couple of beavers on the southeast end of the lake, but Bucky was the only one who ventured this far. Sven had spotted the bristly fellow crossing the road several times.

Bucky finally reached the other side and Sven moved on, Juliette following once again.

He hadn't planned to invite her to dinner. It had just sort of worked out that way. It was logical they'd sit down and discuss the set. He had dinner waiting in a pot. No big deal. The only reason he wouldn't have invited her was if he allowed himself to be freaked out by Alberta and Jenna. He'd be damned if he'd have Jenna, or anyone else, thinking he was afraid of Juliette.

The tall evergreens gave way to a clearing, the lake to the right, cabins to the left. He parked in the graveled space, big enough to accommodate two vehicles, next to the two side-by-side cabins. Juliette pulled into the empty spot beside him. For sure, she drove a sweet ride—a classic Series IIA Land Rover. It was cool as well as functional—a veritable workhorse that could be repaired on the spot in remote locations. There was something to be said for a woman who knew her way around an engine, which she obviously did. Flying a plane into remote areas required she know engine repair. There was something kind of sexy about a woman who could handle those things.

Juliette climbed out of her truck, looking around. A slight breeze ruffled her short, dark hair and carried her scent to him. "It sure is nice out here," she said.

"Yeah, it is. There are some awesome places in Alaska, but Shadow Lake is one of the prettiest I've ever seen." He'd fallen in love with the location the first time he saw it. It was quiet and private without the absolute isolation he'd seen in some parts of the state and even in the surrounding area.

He enjoyed staying in the cabin overlooking the tranquil lake ringed by towering spruce, snowcapped mountains visible in the distance. "Have you been out here before?"

Without discussing it, of one accord, they both walked toward the lake.

"Once for dinner," Juliette said as they skirted a thatch of fireweed in the clearing between the cabins and the water, the purple-pink spires standing thigh high. "It was after Dalton and Skye moved into the new house, which, by the way, is lovely. Your work is quite nice."

They stopped at the lake's edge, the gentle lapping of water against the shore soothing and rhythmic. Dalton and Skye's new home was situated farther down the shore. After dark, the lights would glimmer among the trees.

"Thanks. It was great working on it. Dalton and Skye dig functional, clean design that works with the surroundings." They turned, heading back to the cabins.

"It feels spacious and cozy at the same time."

Her comments pleased him. It felt good to have his work appreciated. "That's exactly what we were aiming for." They walked up onto the porch. "Want to come in or we can sit out here?" He'd opt for the outside any time.

"Out here is nice," she said.

"Take the chair." He motioned to the only seat on the porch. "I'll hold up the railing." He propped on the railing, resting his back against the post. Juliette settled on the kitchen chair he kept on the porch. "Skye didn't cook when you came over, did she?" he asked.

It was common knowledge Skye, while she was a helluva doctor, was a lousy cook. Actually, it was something of an ongoing debate throughout town as to who was worse in the kitchen, Skye or Jenna.

Juliette laughed and Sven realized that in the months he'd known her it was the first time he'd heard her laugh. Her amusement had a musical quality. "No, Dalton cooked. I understand it's best that way. Skye's the first to say she'd starve left to her own devices and no takeout."

He was curious about Juliette. In a town where everyone knew everyone else's business, all he knew of her was that she flew a bush plane and kept to herself. He knew she had short, wavy hair that made his fingers itch to run through it and a mouth that directed his thoughts to long, slow kisses on an

Alaskan spring evening. Other than that, she was a mystery. "What about you? Do you cook?"

She shrugged and offered another one of her quiet smiles. "Nothing gourmet, but I manage." She sniffed. Even with the cabin door closed, the faint aroma of roasted meat and vegetables mingled with the scent of evergreen and fresh air. "You obviously know your way around a kitchen...or at least a Crock-Pot."

Ah, a dry sense of humor lurked beneath that serious, faintly mysterious exterior. "The Crock-Pot is a beautiful thing. My parents were adamant my brother and I know how to take care of ourselves."

"There's a lot to be said for self-sufficiency." A hint of melancholy tinged her smile and shadowed her eyes, and it was as if she retreated a bit into her shell. What had he said wrong?

It was just as he'd known from the get-go—the woman would be a boatload of trouble to figure out, and who needed that?

"Yeah, there is. What do you say we eat out here? I do most evenings. Even if I eat at Gus's I usually wind up out here at some point before I go to bed. Of course, that's since it's warmed up."

"The porch would be fine. I like being outdoors and it's a nice view of the lake and the sky."

"I'll grab dinner."

"Need any help?" She shifted forward as if to get up.

"Nope. I've got it covered." He stopped at the door. "What can I get you to drink? Beer? Milk? Water? I'm not a wine drinker."

"Water sounds good. Are you sure you don't need any help?"

The place was kind of a mess. He wasn't the neatest guy and he almost never had guests. "No. I think I can manage two plates and drinks. Mind if I have a beer?"

"Of course not." There was a hint of searching in her regard, as if she was looking for some deeper meaning.

"I'll be right back then." Sven stepped into the cabin, closing the door behind him. He picked up yesterday's shirt and jeans and tossed them into the bedroom just in case she decided to come in. He did a quick bathroom reconnaissance. Not too bad.

The cabin was essentially one big room with a separate bedroom and bathroom. From the kitchen, where he filled two plates with roast, potatoes and carrots, he could see Juliette through the front window. Even though she looked peaceful enough on the porch, there was a tension in the line of her shoulders.

A loon, with its distinct cry, called from the lake. Dalton had told him the pair returned year after year to spend the summer. Interesting creatures those loons—they mated for life.

He left the plates on the table and carried another

chair outside, Juliette's water glass in his other hand. "Dinner's coming right up."

She took the glass, her fingers brushing his, sending a jolt through him. "Thanks."

He went back in, picked up the plates and utensils and brought them out to the porch. She took her plate and he settled in the empty kitchen chair.

"Hope you enjoy it," Sven said as he automatically tipped his chair back until it rested against the cabin wall.

"It smells delicious," she said, fork in hand.

"Dig in." He loaded his fork with a piece of meat and a potato chunk, suddenly ravenous.

She took a bite and a slow smile lit her brown eyes. "Delicious," she said when she finished chewing and swallowing. "You do know your way around a Crock-Pot."

Inordinately pleased with her compliment, he found he was glad he'd been the one to put that smile on her face. "Glad you like it."

She gestured with her fork, at the vista before them. "I understand why you sit out here most evenings."

The sun slanted onto the covered porch. Sven always thought of this as "the golden hour." Now he stared at Juliette, transfixed by her radiance as the light burnished her hair and skin. Something inside him shifted and fell into place, like when he was notching logs and got the fit just right.

She glanced at him. "Sven?"

He shook his head. What the hell was wrong with him? It had to be that crazy conversation with Jenna. "Uh, yeah. It is a pretty awesome view, isn't it?"

For what could've been one second or minutes, their gazes locked, ensnared. Gold flecked her smoky-brown eyes. His gut tightened and he had the most incredible urge to bridge the space between them and test the smoothness of her skin with his fingertips. Her eyes darkened as if she'd read his desire and wanted the same. Juliette finally looked away.

"So," she prompted, a husky note flavoring her voice that held a Southern undertone. "You had some ideas about the set?" She speared a carrot with her fork, looking at her plate as if the contents fascinated her.

Sven shifted on the hard chair and checked out his own plate rather than the wash of light over her. Meat and potatoes would curb at least one appetite.

Over the meal, he outlined his suggestions and was pleased with her thoughtful comments and questions. Before he knew it, their plates were clean and they'd finished discussing the set.

Juliette stood, her empty plate in hand, "Well, thanks so much for dinner. It was delicious."

The idea that he didn't want her to go flashed through him and instinctively he said, "There's a nice trail down by the lake that leads to a rise with an even better view if you're up for an after-dinner walk."

Surprise registered on her face and she hesitated. Finally she nodded. "That'd be nice."

THE BREEZE BLEW ACROSS the water, cooling Juliette's heated skin and teasing her hair against her neck and temple. She'd been torn. Did she want to soak up more of the tranquillity of Shadow Lake, and the rush of heat and awareness brought on by Sven—feelings she hadn't known in a long time, possibly ever? Or did she want to safely retreat to her own cabin in the woods? She wasn't sure it was the smartest move on her part, but she'd opted to stay.

The path skirted the shore, worn and obviously used by both man and wildlife. She focused on the nuances of the setting rather than the energy radiating from the man beside her—the soothing lapping of water against the shore, the sigh of the wind through the spruce boughs, the muted rhythm of their booted feet against the dirt trail. Mosquitoes, jokingly referred to as Alaska's national bird, buzzed past, and a bald eagle's distant chirping carried on the evening air.

The mosquitoes always reminded her of childhood summers when she'd spent as much time as possible outside. Bug bites had been a small price to pay for a reprieve from the chaos inevitably found indoors.

"So," Sven said, breaking the silence and pulling her back from her brief foray into the past, "how'd you wind up flying a bush plane in Alaska?"

Surely he knew the story. It was a standard question that came with her profession and she'd been asked numerous times. She gave him the same abbreviated, sanitized version everyone else got.

"I've always loved flying, being up in the air."

She was eight years old and once again Mama and Daddy were shouting and throwing things. Juliette darted out the back door when they were distracted. Outside was better than inside, but they could always still find her. She dashed across the field to old man Haddricks's place and scrambled into the cockpit of his crop-duster plane. Her folks never thought to look for her there and she liked to pretend she was flying up in the sky. They couldn't get to her up in the sky.

"All right, little missy," old man Haddricks said, nearly startling the pee out of her. "I been watching you sit in my plane going on near a month. I'm about to dust the Oglesby soybean fields." He hooked his thumbs in the straps of his overalls. His gray, bristling eyebrows nearly met one another over his nose and he never smiled, but his eyes were kind. You could see meanness in a person and it wasn't in him. "You wanna tag along?"

She nodded mutely. Her heart nearly thumping out of her chest, she climbed over into the second seat and buckled in. The next thing she knew, they were off the ground. And for the first time in her life she actually felt safe. It was just like she'd dreamed it would be. No one could find her and no one could harm her when she was in the sky.

She shrugged. "I became a flight attendant, fell in love with Alaska on a long layover and decided to get my pilot's license."

Her life sounded so nice and neat and compartmentalized when in fact it had been one big mess and even that CliffsNotes version dredged it all up for her again. Marrying Boyd Feldman, her high school boyfriend, when she was seventeen just to get out of her parents' house. Foolishly believing Boyd would stand between her and her parents. Realizing she'd jumped from the frying pan into the fire. Divorced by nineteen. Lucking into the flight attendant job. Falling into a second marriage where once again she thought he'd have her back, only to discover the only thing they had in common was burying their respective troubles in a bottle. A second divorce. Waking up in a hotel room one morning after a flight and an evening spent in the hotel bar, not remembering where she was or how she'd gotten there, *knowing* if she didn't make some changes she'd surely ruin her life and die young. Alcoholism was suicide by installment plan.

She'd climbed out of bed, bleary-eyed, hungover and generally mad at the world and gone online and found an AA meeting. She wasn't sure what had been harder, showing up or admitting she was, in fact, the very thing she'd always despised about her parents. An alcoholic.

With sobriety had come the acknowledgment that while being a flight attendant put her in the sky, what she really longed to do was fly a plane.

She'd had a small nest egg set aside, but she'd still busted her butt waiting tables in an all-night diner in Anchorage. It had taken her twice as long to save up the money for flight school because her tips were easily half of what they would've been in a bar. But getting sober and staying sober had been as important as earning her wings.

She certainly didn't lay all that out on the table for Sven, who probably couldn't handle it even if she wanted to tell him…and she didn't. Instead, she simply smiled and said, "And the rest, as they say, is history."

A twig snapped underfoot, underscoring her story.

Sven looked at her as if he could see through all she'd said to the pieces she'd left out, which was unexpected and caught her off guard. And there was something in his look that said he'd ask. "So, you've been flying how long?"

She breathed a sigh of relief, but sooner or later he'd probe. She sensed his curiosity. Most of the time her wall of reserve kept people at bay, but with him…

"Two years now."

Three years and forty-four days of sobriety, and she never, ever took it for granted. She looked up at the ribbons of orange and pink streaking the sky as the sun began its nightly journey toward the horizon. A sense of contentment wove through her.

"I'm never as happy as when I'm up there." The moment those words slipped past her lips she caught herself. Sven was easy to be around in a way she hadn't experienced with anyone before.

"What is it about being up there that you like so much?"

Once again she lowered her guard as if lulled by the place and the man and the moment. "It's freedom and open space and safety."

They climbed the last of a small rise where a stone outcropping formed a natural bench at the top. Without stopping to discuss it, they settled on the sun-warmed rock overlooking the vista of lake, mountain and sinking sun. Fireweed, her favorite Alaskan wildflower, filled a meadow on the far side of the lake. In the distance Dalton and Skye's house sat in the clearing at the edge of the spruce forest. It was all singularly spectacular. She liked the solidness of the stone beneath her.

The wind shifted and Sven's scent wafted around her. He radiated energy, but it wasn't the frenetic mix some people gave off. There was simply a heat and power to him that drew her.

"Open space and safety," he echoed her words. "That's a different take." Sven grinned and pushed his blond hair behind one ear. Juliette noticed a small hole in his earlobe, as if once upon a time he'd sported an earring. Somehow it seemed to fit. He struck her as free-spirited and a little unconventional with his long hair and outgoing personality. She was finding, however, that one-on-one he was quieter than she'd expected.

"Lots of people would find being up in a small plane in a small cockpit in the air confining and somewhat dangerous," he continued.

Dangerous? Danger came in all shapes, forms, sizes and situations. In his own way, Sven was dangerous. Good Lord but he was a sexy, good-looking hunk of man. And how had she been around him for months and not noticed he had a dimple when he smiled? Probably because she'd always been careful to never look directly at him. A general nod in his direction and a vague hello and she'd kept moving. She'd never been in his direct line of fire.

His blue eyes crinkled at the corners and that dimple came into play. It made her glad she was supported by a solid surface because neither her pulse nor her legs felt particularly steady.

Cough up an answer, Juliette. Oh, yeah, small plane and dangerous… "Different perspectives,

I guess." And she was done talking about herself.
"How did you get into building?" It wasn't just a
change of subject. She wanted to know.

"I always liked doing things with my hands." He
held his hands up. They were the hands of a working man—broad with calluses across the palms. "I
like making things. I enjoy physical labor. Pops has
an accounting business and my brother works with
him. I know he wanted me to join the company, but
I could never sit behind a desk and push a pen, it's
just not my thing."

"Your family's okay with that?"

"They'd have been disappointed if it was Eric, but
me…nah."

She didn't know him well—in fact, she didn't
know him at all, she simply knew *of* him and that
was in passing—but without a doubt he wasn't cut
out to be a pen pusher behind a desk.

"The summer I was fourteen I worked with this
guy down the street who was a builder. After that I
worked with him every summer. When I graduated
high school I went with him full-time. It was really
a lot like having an apprenticeship. It's the same me-
chanics but no two jobs are the same. I get to travel
where the work takes me, meet new people—" he
offered a carefree shrug "—it's all good."

A smile curved his sensuous mouth, lit his blue
eyes and Juliette wondered if there was a woman

alive who could resist this man if he set his mind to truly charming her.

She'd never quite figured out why he and Jenna hadn't wound up together. Jenna had married an old high school crush who'd turned up in Good Riddance, but what about before that? In fact, almost all happenings were public knowledge and she'd never heard of any "happenings" between Sven and anyone.

It was the public-knowledge bit that had kept her uninvolved in the time she'd been here—plus, she'd been busy building her flying business and getting her life in order. And there'd been the little matter that she didn't *want* to get involved with a man. She simply wasn't interested, or even remotely tempted. Until now. Now she was sitting right next to temptation.

He slid his hand across the stone and traced the path of a blue vein in the back of her hand with his fingertip. One simple, innocuous touch from him and Juliette felt as if a dam had burst inside her. Want, need, desire tore through her.

"Juliette, would you like to go to dinner with me one evening or maybe hiking one afternoon?"

She felt as if she couldn't breathe. Panic rushed in, chasing the other torrent. "We just had dinner and went for a hike."

"I mean, like a date." And still he tortured her senses with the drag of his fingertip against her skin.

She snatched her hand away. Coming here had been a mistake. Opening herself up had been a mistake. What had she been thinking? She hadn't—that was the problem. But she was fully thinking now.

She stood. "Thanks, but I don't think so. I can find my way back."

4

SVEN SAT AND WATCHED Juliette's trim, khaki-clad derriere disappear down the trail. What the hell had just happened? Part of him wanted to just let her sashay off into the sunset—literally. However, Marge Sorenson had reared him strictly. His mother would maintain that since Sven had invited Juliette out here as his guest, it was his duty to see her off. Plus, he wanted to know what he had done. He hadn't planned to ask her out, but they were having a good time and he was enjoying her company and so he'd rolled with it.

He started down the trail. She had a head start, but his legs were longer. The loon's call across the water seemed to mock him and he shook his head. Damn it all to hell. Was he right or was he right?

She was definitely, decidedly, without a doubt too much trouble. One minute he touched the back of her hand with his finger and asked her on an official date. The next second she was vamoosing down the bunny trail, all freaked out. It wasn't as if he'd made a pass at her or been lewd or any of the other sins men committed against women. He'd touched her hand and asked her out. Jeez Louise.

He caught a glimpse of her ahead of him. "Wait up, Juliette," he called out. He might walk fast, but he drew the line at running after her.

She stopped and waited. When he'd almost caught up to her, she resumed walking. "I told you I could find my way back." Her tone was neutral.

He strove for an equally bland tone. "You're here as my guest. I'll see you back."

She nodded without breaking stride. "Okay."

He didn't know how else to handle the situation so he just threw it out there. "I'm not sure what happened back there, but I didn't mean to offend you or overstep boundaries."

She slowed her steps. "You didn't offend me. I simply think it's best if we keep things on a strictly business level."

"Why?" If she wasn't attracted to him, he could certainly handle that, but that wasn't at all what he'd felt, what he'd seen in her eyes. "What are you afraid of?"

"I'm not…" She petered out, looking away from him once again but not before he'd seen a flicker of trepidation cross her face. "It's just less complicated that way."

Really, *it* wasn't. The situation itself was pretty straightforward. She was attracted to him. He was attracted to her. Nope, *she* was the complicated factor. And yeah, it'd be easy to just let it and her go and roll on along his merry way. However, for the first time ever, he found he didn't want to go the easy route. He found he couldn't let her walk away. "You know what I think?"

"I'm not interested in what you think," she said without hostility.

He was running on gut instinct and he didn't believe her. "Yes, you are." He caught her arm in his hand and they both stopped. He turned her to face him. He wasn't so egotistical that he couldn't accept that a woman wasn't attracted to him. However, he'd been around the block enough to know when a woman was, and she might not be happy about it, but she was as attracted to him as he was to her. She could easily shake off his hand and walk away. She didn't.

Wariness marked her expression in the gloaming light. He drew her to him. "I think you're afraid of this."

As he lowered his head, she parted her lips. They were soft, her breath sweet, as she met his kiss.

JULIETTE'S EYES FLUTTERED closed. She'd been kissed, but she'd never been kissed like this. His mouth was firm and giving, his kiss tender.

She wound her arms around his neck, his hair brushing against the backs of her hands, his nape warm beneath her palms. He wrapped his arms around her, pulling her closer. Instinctively, she leaned into him, heat rushing through her. He tasted good; he felt better.

She wasn't sure if it was her or him, although she thought it was both of them, who deepened the kiss. Scorching heat and searing want arced between them. His body pressing into hers, she tangled her tongue with his, drawn to him despite all sound reasoning. Her breasts ached against his chest. Her thighs dampened, aroused by the press of his burgeoning hardness against her. The press of his broad hands against her back…the heat of his skin…his scent…

Slowly, sanity crept back into her brain. She pulled away and stepped back, running her hands through her hair, trying desperately to find her composure. He'd stripped away her defenses with one, not-so-simple kiss.

A loon cried in the distance, mosquitoes hummed and their ragged breathing hung on the evening air.

Finally, Juliette found her voice. "Yes," she said. She sounded rusty. Swallowing, she continued, "That's exactly what I'm afraid of."

It had been everything she'd feared kissing him might be. It had rocked through her and left her wanting more.

Sven smoothed his hair back with a slightly unsteady hand. "I thought it was pretty awesome."

Somewhere inside she was glad she hadn't been the only one. "It was."

"And that's problematic?"

Problematic? How about it scared the hell out of her? She'd made two major man mistakes in the past. She'd been doing good since she'd quit drinking, her life was on an even keel. Rocking the boat was a frightening prospect—and she knew, perhaps she'd known from the first time she'd seen him, that there was something about Sven Sorenson that could rock her boat. That kiss just proved it. Her boat was definitely feeling the impact of that kiss.

She wrapped her arms around her middle, looking past him to the stand of trees visible over his shoulder. "I don't want to get involved with anyone."

"I asked you on a date. I kissed you." She could practically feel his perplexity. "I didn't say I wanted to be involved."

Part of getting sober had been a commitment to living her life honestly—being honest with herself and others, but it didn't mean she had to lay out every aspect of her life for scrutiny. On the other hand, he struck her as one of the few genuinely nice guys and she didn't want to hurt his feelings. "Look, it's not personal." And in a weird way, it wasn't. It was about her, not him. "I just can't do this."

"Sure." He started walking again and she automatically matched her stride to his. "No problem."

Obviously he was taking it personally. She knew how to send him running as fast as possible from her. She didn't bandy about her personal business, but her gut told her whatever she said to Sven would stay between them. Sven had a bit of a reputation as a pretty carefree, laid-back guy and she got the impression some people thought he was a bit of a lightweight, but she didn't think that was the case at all. She suspected there was more to Sven Sorenson than people thought. Instinct told her he wouldn't pass her business around Good Riddance.

She drew a deep breath and plunged in without preamble. "Look, Sven, I'm an alcoholic." He stopped abruptly. She halted walking but kept talking. "I've been married and divorced twice. My baggage would fill the cargo area of my plane and then some."

Surprise bordering on shock etched his features. "You're an alkie?" He caught himself. "Damn. Sorry. I meant an alcoholic. But I've never even seen you drink."

"Because I'm a sober alkie," she said dryly.

A frown furrowed his forehead. "But you fly."

"Exactly." God, this was uncomfortable. Going to a meeting or talking with her sponsor was one thing, but she hated discussing it with an "outsider." "I don't exactly advertise it because I am a pilot—" *and there were so many misperceptions and prejudices out there* "—but Merrilee and Bull know." She'd only thought it fair that Merrilee know up front before she hired Juliette, and Bull had been part of the hiring process, as well. Merrilee had been gracious, understanding and willing to take a chance. Bull had simply nodded. Merrilee had hired Juliette, and the subject had never been mentioned again. Juliette felt certain the couple had never shared that information with anyone else. "I haven't had a drink in over three years…one thousand one hundred thirty-nine days, to be precise."

They continued down the trail. "Congratulations, then," he said. "I'm sorry I had the beer tonight—"

She cut him off. "If it would've been a problem, I would've said so. It's not."

That was one reason she kept the truth to herself. She didn't want people tiptoeing around her, treating her as if she was fragile or some time bomb waiting to explode.

She felt him peer at her. "Is that why you don't hang out at Gus's? I've noticed you come in and eat sometimes, but you never hang out, and I've never seen you at karaoke night."

She smiled. "There are definitely better places for a sober drunk to hang out than a bar. But I don't particularly like crowds, and I can't carry a tune in a bucket, so no, karaoke night isn't my thing."

Sven chuckled and she realized things felt relaxed

between them. "You can always count on a crowd at Gus's."

It was a relief to have actually said it to him, and that he'd rolled with it. "Yes, you can."

He whistled beneath his breath. "Two husbands… and you're how old?"

Juliette was so startled she laughed. "Not shy or even polite, are you?"

"Not particularly," he said. She caught a flash of his white teeth in the burgeoning dark.

She couldn't even be offended when it was the same way she felt. Two ex-husbands before she'd even hit twenty-nine—that wasn't such a great track record. "Obviously you never heard that you're not supposed to ask women their age. I'm thirty-two. How old are you?"

"Thirty." She'd speculated somewhere between thirty and thirty-three. "Any kids?"

Once again, his blunt questions surprised her. He wasn't nearly as predictable as she'd thought he'd be. She laughed. "Do you see any kids?"

He shrugged. "Just asking. Kids aren't always with their parents."

She'd been ever so thankful that she'd had the good sense not to procreate in either of her disastrous marriages. The way things were going, it looked as if children weren't in her future. The thought sometimes left an ache inside her, but most of the time she simply didn't think about it. And that might've had something to do with her decision to send a gift to Jenna's shower instead of showing up for the event.

And what was good for the goose was good for the gander. "What about you? You have any kids?"

"Not yet. I'm a pretty conventional guy—you know, a wife first, one day. So, you want to vent about your ex-husbands?"

Once again, he startled her into amusement. "Thanks, but I'm good. They're in the past."

"No, they're not."

She walked past his cabin and the one next door to her truck. She crossed her arms over her chest. Shadows obscured his face. He was so big he should've seemed ominous in the dark, but she felt totally comfortable, although somewhat annoyed by his smug assertion. "Really? It appears to me they're in the past."

"Then your perspective is skewed."

"Please, enlighten me."

"Oh, no, darlin', I'd say you've very much brought them with you into the present, otherwise they wouldn't be a problem, would they?" He paused and when she had nothing to say—because really there was nothing to say to that—he continued. "What were their names?"

"Boyd and Derrick," she answered automatically. He had a way of throwing out things—questions, comments, opinions—that rattled her composure. "Why? What difference does it make?"

"I was just curious. So, did you change your last name after your last divorce? I know some women go back to their maiden name."

"No. I really didn't see the point." She'd been Juliette Kincaid for her first seventeen years and she hadn't liked herself or her life very much in that time frame, so she'd had no interest in revisiting that name. They had so exhausted this topic. "Thanks for dinner, and it was a nice hike." It had actually been a nice evening—and a helluva kiss—but she wasn't about to add a thank-you for that last part.

"I enjoyed your company. Very much. And the hike. And the kiss."

Leave it to Sven to include that kiss.

He leaned in and her heart thumped in her chest like a wild animal in flight…or heat was more like it. She could feel his energy, his fire, and her own responded in kind. She knew she should turn away, she should take flight, but she simply stood there.

He dropped a chaste kiss against her forehead and straightened. "Good night, Juliette Miller. Drive safe. I'll see you tomorrow night."

He turned on his heel and walked away, melding into the night, his boots crunching against the gravel. She yanked open her door and climbed into the driver's seat.

The featherlight brush of his lips against her forehead packed as much impact, in its own way, as their earlier kiss. And his assertion he'd see her tomorrow night held more of a note of promise than an appointment.

What had they started?

SVEN KILLED THE WATER and climbed out of the shower. He toweled dry. pulled on a pair of briefs and headed to his sketch pad. Ever since Juliette's taillights had faded down the driveway, a restlessness had gripped him. The shower had helped, but it was as if his equilibrium was still off.

The feel of her in his arms, the taste of her mouth, the seductive velvet of her tongue—he wanted those things again. He wanted her. And she was even more problematic than he'd anticipated. Two husbands? He had enough sense to know she'd told him that to scare him off. Damn straight, any man in his right mind would dodge that bullet. And he had yet to meet a woman who didn't want to say what an asshole her last husband or boyfriend was. What the hell was wrong with her? Toss in that she couldn't hold her booze and yeah—that particular combo of woman ought to screw up any guy's wet dream. Which led him right back to his creed—women were best uncomplicated.

So, why was he sitting here doodling, her shape taking form on vellum with a piece of charcoal?

Across the room, his cell phone rang from where

he'd left it on the counter. He crossed the room and answered, surprised she'd waited this long to call.

"You still up?" his mother asked without preamble. Whereas Sven was simply a night owl, Marge Sorenson was an insomniac. It had made for a lot of mother-son time when he was still living at home and they were the only two in the household still awake at 1:00 a.m. Now their late-night chats a couple of times a week were as much habit as anything.

They covered the cursory small talk. He listened with half an ear as she relayed the antics of his pops babysitting Sven's niece that afternoon. His mother loved dissecting the minutiae of a day. She would've been the perfect candidate for the endless updates posted on all the social media, except his mom didn't dig computers. Sven couldn't say he was big into them, either.

"So, I heard Bull broke his arm and you're working with the dinner theater production."

Sven had been in Good Riddance for the past ten months, but his folks were practically honorary citizens. They'd missed Chrismoose last year because their first, make that only, grandchild had just been born, but other than that they didn't miss the weeklong, annual pre-Christmas festival in Good Riddance. Chrismoose had devotees far and wide in Alaska. Long before he'd picked up work in the small town, his folks had been coming during the holiday season. His mom and Merrilee had hit it off like a house afire. He was pretty sure that was one of the reasons he'd gotten the contract on Jenna's spa, not that his work couldn't stand on its own merit, but... Obviously Marge and Merrilee had conversed this evening.

"I have."

"Oh, good. That should be fun. Maybe Pops and I should come up for the play."

"Sure. That'd be great." The thought crossed his mind that his folks would like Juliette. Of course, short of someone being Attila the Hun, his folks pretty much liked everyone, which was probably why Sven and his brother were the same way. Never meet a stranger. Always look a person in the eye. Offer up a strong handshake. That was the Sorenson way.

"I heard that...oh, I can't remember her name... that pretty bush pilot was out at your place tonight." Inquisitive speculation was evident in his mom's voice.

He wasn't a bit surprised his mother had that information at her disposal. "She was."

"What's her name again?"

His mom never forgot a face, but she was terrible with names. "Juliette. Juliette Miller."

"I see."

Huh? She sounded as if she'd just uncovered a state secret. "You see what?"

"I see you're interested in her."

He glanced at the charcoal sketch of Juliette and walked over to the fridge. "And what would lead you to that conclusion?"

"You're my chatty child." He was a thirty-year-old man, but he didn't bother to correct the child bit. He snagged the milk jug and drank, not bothering with a glass. "But you haven't said a word about her. And it was the way you said her name."

"She's...different." He leaned against the counter.

"Yeah?" He heard the rustling on the other end of the line and knew his mom was settling on the sofa. "Tell me about her. How's she different?"

He rolled through Juliette's standoffish demeanor and the fact that she was a bush pilot and drove one of the coolest trucks he'd ever seen. He left out that simply sitting near her put him in the grips of something he'd never felt before. He'd known lust, but never this...compulsion. And that wasn't the kind of thing a guy would say to his mom.

"Where's she from?" Marge sounded intrigued. He knew the feeling.

That was public knowledge. "Someplace in North Carolina. She lived in Anchorage while she got her pilot's license. She was a flight attendant before that."

"Alaska's a long way from North Carolina. What about her family?"

Pops's parents were fifty miles from Wasilla and

Marge's were half a block away from his folks' place. "I don't know."

"She ever been married?"

He hesitated. It really wasn't his business to tell and it was obviously something that wasn't common knowledge or he'd have known before she told him tonight…and his mom would already have known even before him.

Marge was a sharp one. "How many times?" Apparently his hesitation had spoken volumes.

"Twice." He waited. His mom wasn't judgmental, but she held marriage forth as the most sacred of vows, which probably accounted for him being thirty and unwed. He'd never run across anyone he felt he wanted to wake up to for the rest of his life, and he'd been reared to believe that when you crossed the matrimonial threshold, that was what you were signing on for. For better or for worse. In sickness and in health. The whole spiel including till death do we part. A serious commitment that required a rock-solid foundation.

"And that's not common knowledge," he added. He had to give his mom credit. She'd keep it to herself. Even though they were tight, Merrilee wouldn't hear it from Marge.

"Hmm. And what is it you're not telling me?"

"Nothing."

"You've always been a terrible liar. That's why you're such a lousy poker player."

"I'm not a lousy poker player." Actually, he sucked at poker, but it was still fun.

"Right. So, there's something you're not saying."

His mother didn't miss much. "It's not my place to tell the rest, Mom."

"Sven Sorenson, you know I won't tell a soul if you ask me not to."

He did know that, but she would still know and it wasn't his story to tell. "I know that, Mom, but you'll meet her when you come and—"

"Has she had one of those sex changes like Donna?" Donna, who ran Good Riddance's small-engine repair business, used to be Don, back in the day.

"No. Juliette's not transgender."

"She was a prostitute?"

Marge was tripping. "Not to my knowledge."

"Stripper? Not that I'm judging. A woman has to make a living."

He couldn't imagine Juliette on a pole. "Mom."

"She did jail time?"

"She couldn't hold a pilot's license if she was a felon."

Sven was torn. Marge wasn't short on imagination. He'd been pushing her for years to write a book. His mother would keep filling in the blanks with wild speculation. The truth wasn't nearly as out there as what she'd come up with.

"She's an alcoholic."

"Oh. Oh, dear."

He didn't know what he expected, but it wasn't that note of dismay. It kind of rubbed him the wrong way.

"She hasn't had a drink in over three years."

"Oh, honey. I can tell you find her interesting, but you need to just be friends." Her tone said she'd pat him sympathetically on the head if he was standing in front of her. "You know there'd always be the chance she'd relapse and that would be hard to deal with. Worse yet, that disease is hereditary. That's not something you'd want to wish on your kids."

His kids? Damn, he'd only had her out to dinner. His mom was putting the cart way before the horse. Nonetheless, resentment swelled inside him on Juliette's behalf. He understood now why she kept to herself and kept her secret just that.

5

ABOUT TEN MINUTES OUT, Juliette radioed for clearance and Merrilee's voice crackled back with an affirmative.

"Almost there," Juliette said to Logan Jeffries, her last "cargo" for the day. "I'm sure you're ready to be home."

Logan, Jenna's husband, spent one week of every month in Atlanta at his family business's headquarters. The rest of the time, he telecommuted from Good Riddance.

"Definitely. I'm ready to see my wife. Thank goodness the baby didn't decide on an early arrival while his or her daddy was on the other side of the country."

"How much longer is it? When's the baby due?" There'd been a shower a couple of months ago and she'd sent a gift, but she didn't really keep up with stuff like that.

"The middle of next month. That's why this is the final trip for a while. I was a nervous wreck the entire time I was there."

It was extraordinary really—Logan had been fairly reserved, maybe a tad stuffy, when he'd shown up in Good Riddance last October. She supposed it was the town and his wife's influence that he was far more open now. The Logan Jeffries of old would've never confided being nervous. Actually, he would've never confided about anything. He was a walking, talking poster child for the transforming power of love.

They circled the small town and Juliette started to descend. "Are you enjoying the new house and adapting to the new business?" He and Jenna lived above the spa. Lots of proprietors in town lived adjacent to or above their business.

Logan smiled. "I'm glad we got into the house and she got the business rolling in the new location before the baby came. Moving was a pain, but we love the place. Sven did a great job. I hear he's working with you on the play now. Nice guy, huh?"

"He seems very nice."

"The first time I met him was when he plopped down in Gus's and told Jenna they needed to decide what they were going to do in the bedroom." He chuckled. "I wasn't quite sure what to think."

Juliette tamped down a moment of totally irrational jealousy. Sven was an inveterate flirt. But she could certainly see where Logan would've been non-plussed. "Were you worried?"

"I'll have to say for a minute I wondered. I just couldn't imagine any man not being half in love with Jenna." Juliette would second that. Jenna was gorgeous and outgoing and the kind of woman you'd love to hate, if she just wasn't so darn sweet and big-hearted. "And isn't he what you women call a hunk?"

It took Juliette a second to realize Logan was actually asking her; the question wasn't merely rhetorical. "Um, yeah, I guess he is sort of a hunk."

That was like saying Mount Everest was a hill. She couldn't imagine there was a woman alive whose pulse wouldn't pound if they simply shared breathing space with Sven Sorenson.

"I'm glad he wasn't interested in Jenna because that would've been some stiff competition."

Juliette smiled and felt a tug of wistfulness inside her. Jenna Rathburne Jeffries was so obviously head over heels in love with her husband it was both inspiring and painful to witness. "It doesn't seem as if you have any competition where Jenna's concerned."

Logan's grin verged on goofy. He was equally smitten with his wife. "Yeah, that's pretty cool, huh? I'd say I'm about the luckiest guy on the planet."

It'd be nice to have someone feel that way about her, but she just didn't think those cards were in the hand she'd been dealt, so she was simply playing her own game of solitaire. And happy to do so.

Juliette brought the plane down, braked to a stop and killed the engine. "I'd say you and Jenna are both pretty lucky...and that baby." A longing stirred inside her for the family she'd never had. Oh, she'd technically had a family, but somewhere within was the yearning for that Hallmark-card home unit, not the dysfunctional wreckage she'd grown up with. She'd just accepted, after her childhood and her subsequent disastrous marriages, that what Jenna and Logan had, with baby about to make three, simply wasn't in the cards for her.

"Yeah, we are." Logan opened the door and started climbing out. "Thanks for the ride," he said with a smile as he swung his travel bag over his shoulder and set off with a long stride. "I'm going to check on my family," he said over his shoulder. "Tell Sven I said hello."

What? Was she the man's messenger service now? She pasted on a smile and called out, "Will do. Give Jenna my regards, as well." She hadn't seen Jenna in a couple of days, but then Jenna had been wrapped up in the spa and Juliette was plenty busy with her job and the set. Flights were always up this time of year with the influx of tourists and folks coming out for fishing and backpacking.

Juliette crossed to the air terminal door and walked in. Merrilee, sitting behind her desk, looked unusually harried.

"Hi, Juliette. I swear it'll be the first time anyone ever dies from a broken arm."

Juliette had to bite her lower lip to keep from laughing. Merrilee was so seldom out of sorts, and hardly ever with Bull, but this was obviously about Bull as he was the only person in town with a broken arm. "What's wrong?"

"I may kill him just to put us both out of our misery if he's this kind of patient the entire time."

Juliette simply smiled. Merrilee and Bull were devoted to one another without being sickening. Sort of like Jenna and Logan...and Nelson and Ellie...and Clint and Tessa...and Dalton and Skye...and Petey and Donna...and well, the list seemed rather endless these days. It was almost enough to give a sensible woman foolish thoughts of happy-ever-after not just being a pipe dream.

"Sorry things are so iffy," Juliette said. "I hope Bull shapes up. Curl's pretty busy with his taxidermy business now. Having to move into mortuary mode now would throw him for a loop."

"You're probably right. If Curl had to take care of a human dead body during the middle of tourist and taxidermy season, that'd throw a kink in his hosepipe. I'll give Bull another day to pull himself out of his doldrums. I've suggested he collaborate with Sven, but no, he's got to sulk. Says he's not interested in armchair quarterbacking." She shook her head in disgust and then waved a hand as if dismissing Bull. "How'd it go with Sven last night?"

Talk about a loaded question. Juliette, however, took it at face value. "Fine. He gets the design concept and he had a couple of good suggestions."

Merrilee nodded, satisfaction in her smile. "I knew he would. He's a nice guy."

They'd covered that last night. Why was everyone suddenly intent on waxing eloquent about what a great guy Sven Sorenson was? She got it. She concurred. "Yes, he is." And a heck of a kisser. In fact, she'd lain awake for hours reliving that kiss—still tingling, her thoughts and emotions tangling around her until the wee hours of the morning. She'd longed for the touch of his broad hands against her skin, the feel of his mouth against her neck, the scrape of his teeth against her flesh, the stroke of his tongue against her.

Mr. Isn't-He-A-Great-Guy Sorenson had been singularly responsible for the dark circles under her eyes this morning. And that more than proved her point that it was best to walk her path alone. It was far less complicated. And she wasn't fond of sleepless nights tossing and turning in some ridiculous fever of want brought on by one, well, technically two, kisses.

"His mom and dad booked a table for the play today. They're coming."

Why in the world would that set off a storm of

anxiety in the pit of her stomach? On multiple fronts the man was shaking her up, both directly and indirectly.

"Oh, good. I'm…uh…I hope they enjoy it."

"Oh, Marge and Edgar will love it. And you'll love them. They're good people. Marge is over the moon with her first grandbaby, Tanya—Sven's brother, Eric, and his wife, Darnita, had a baby right before Christmas. They're crazy about that kid."

Couples in love…babies…families…it all seemed to be smacking her in the face suddenly. "That's nice."

She didn't really know what else to say. But she was getting the picture that the Sorensons were one big happy family of love and joy and tranquillity. She'd bet her bottom dollar none of them had ever broken all the dishes in the cupboard in a drunken rage while their kid looked on.

Not that she wanted anything to do with her own dysfunctional familial unit, but people like the Sorensons always made her a little uncomfortable. It was as if they were all wearing clean white T-shirts while she had a big greasy stain smeared down the front of hers. She preferred to keep her dirty laundry to herself.

She'd thought more than once that it would've been nice to have parents like Merrilee and Bull. Juliette had the feeling they'd have her back if she needed them, especially Merrilee.

"Be prepared to ooh and aah over baby pictures, because Marge doesn't go anywhere without her Nana Brag Book."

"Thanks for the heads-up." This entire conversation made her uncomfortable. She didn't want to know Sven's parents were named Marge and Edgar. She didn't want to know about Eric, Darnita and their cute bundle of joy, Tanya.

She wanted Sven to remain just another person she saw in passing, just another resident who was handling the set design along with her. She didn't want the details about his happy family. She didn't want to be reminded that she'd never fit into that kind of dynamic. How could she, even if she wanted to? She had no experience with that.

Merrilee reached to the table situated behind her and picked up a muffin with a napkin. "Here's a carrot-raisin-bran muffin. Eat it. I know you're not going to have time for dinner before rehearsal."

That was the kind of thing she loved about Merrilee. "Thanks. I think I am kind of hungry." It had taken a while to get used to Merrilee's mothering ways without feeling slightly smothered, but now it just felt good. Juliette simply hadn't been used to anyone giving a damn whether or not she ate a meal or had a bed to sleep in.

She bit into the muffin. It was the perfect blend of sweet carrots, plump raisins and hearty bran. "Yum."

"Have another one." Merrilee was already reaching behind her.

Juliette held up her hand. "This is fine. I'd better run or I'm going to be late."

"Enjoy your weekend off."

"Will do."

"Got plans?"

"I'm going to work on some wind chimes that have been knocking around in my head."

Making chimes freed her mind and her spirit— the second-best thing to being up in the sky itself. Just her and her wind chimes and it would put Sven Sorenson firmly out of her mind because there was simply no place for Sven in her mind…or her life… and certainly not in her heart.

HEAVINESS WEIGHED DOWN Merrilee's heart. Bull, his arm in a sling, pushed through the door and interrupted her melancholy. "Why the long face? Other than you're aggravated with me?"

She ran her finger over her lower lip, contemplating the woman who'd just walked out the front door. "Juliette…" Merrilee shook her head. "I don't know. I can't help but worry about her."

Bull snagged a muffin and settled in the empty chair next to Merrilee's desk. "Some people just keep to themselves, Merrilee. You know that by now. God knows, we see our share of them here in Alaska."

She poured him a cup of coffee—black—and passed it to him. He nodded in appreciation, his mouth full of muffin.

"I know. And see, that's the problem. I know how those people feel. It's like they give off a certain energy. They really are perfectly content being an island unto themselves." Still chewing, Bull nodded. "And I'd be fine with it if that's the feeling I got from Juliette, but it's not. I think that girl has surrounded herself with a thick wall of isolation to protect herself."

"Nothing, huh?"

Juliette confounded and concerned Merrilee. "Two years she's worked for me. From her employment application I know she's from North Carolina. She lived in Raleigh for a while, then Anchorage. Her emergency contact is a woman named Sue Dickens in Anchorage. The only bit of personal information outside of that employment record is that her yard is full of wind chimes and whirligigs and she's an air sign."

"Huh?"

"An air sign. You know. She's a Libra."

In the middle of chasing his muffin with coffee, Bull rolled his eyes at her. Merrilee rolled her eyes back at him and forged ahead. "It makes sense. She flies, she's into wind chimes and whirligigs, she's a thinker… She's an air sign."

"Sure. Okay."

Talking about astrology always earned an eye roll from Bull. The man was obtuse and stubborn. Merrilee had shown him how perfectly *their* signs aligned but he remained a skeptic. She didn't dare tell him Alberta had shared her psychic matchmaking and that the traveling Gypsy had confided Sven and Juliette were meant for one another. Bull liked Alberta, but he didn't give her psychic abilities much weight. However, much like astrology, Merrilee had found Alberta to be pretty darned on the money. Hadn't she told Merrilee back in the day Bull was the man for her? That had certainly turned out right enough. But he'd have to convince himself; she was done trying. She moved on conversationally to less esoteric ground.

"Marge is worried. She's afraid Juliette's going to break Sven's heart."

Bull bristled on Juliette's behalf. That's why Merrilee was still so hopelessly in love with him after twenty-five years. "She's not that kind of woman."

"Oh, she wouldn't break his heart on purpose. In fact, if she thought he was offering his heart, it'd probably scare her to death. Marge is worried about Juliette's previous marriages. I have a feeling she knows about Juliette's alcoholism as well, but I could hardly betray Juliette's confidence by asking, and if Marge does know she would've been told in confidence. So, I think she knows, but I couldn't bring it up and if she does know she couldn't bring it up, so it wasn't brought up. Regardless, I think the real issue is whether Juliette will allow herself to care about someone. And I don't think I've ever seen anyone more in need of being loved than that girl."

"Gus?"

"Even more than Gus. Gus had good years with her mother before she lost her. And the situation with Troy was terrible and frightening, but she knew her mother's love." Her goddaughter, Gus, had sought sanctuary in Good Riddance from an abusive, stalking fiancé a couple of years earlier. Gus had been traumatized, but she at least had a solid foundation under her that Merrilee didn't think Juliette had ever known. "It's more of what Juliette doesn't say than what she does that leads me to believe she had a fairly dismal childhood."

"Honey, you can't fix everyone's problems."

"I know. But I can't seem to stop trying."

"Then you're about to be as happy as a pig in a mud pit. I walked over to tell you I got an email from my sister."

Bull was so removed from his sister, most of the time Merrilee forgot he had one. "Janie?"

"I only have the one." He never said what had happened between them and she never asked. If and when he wanted to tell, he'd tell. "My nephew Liam is heading this way."

They hadn't seen Janie or her boys, twins Liam and Lars and the baby, Jack, in years. They only knew what was going on with them through occasional updates from Bull's brother.

"Oh, my goodness. When is he expected to arrive?"

"No idea. I just know he's on his way. He got on his motorcycle and rolled out yesterday."

Merrilee could do flexible. It helped to have time to prepare for visiting family, even if it was family they hadn't seen in—she did a quick mental calculation—sixteen or so years. Liam had been fifteen or sixteen when they'd come out one summer. "He's home on leave?" The last they'd heard he was in the army. "How long is he going to stay?"

"He's out of the military."

"Out?"

Bull nodded. "Done. And he's not just visiting. Janie says he's moving here."

Merrilee wasn't sure what to say. There was certainly more going on here than met the eye. "He's just bringing himself and his motorcycle and he's staying? I'll hand it to him that he's traveling light."

Bull nodded. "You know how Janie likes to be cryptic, but apparently he left the service on a medical discharge. Another lost lamb for your fold."

Despite his comment, Merrilee knew Bull was concerned about his nephew. Bull just wasn't going to wear his feelings on his sleeve the way Merrilee did…nor did she want him to. That was her job in their relationship.

ALBERTA FELL INTO STEP beside Sven as he walked toward the community center.

"What's shaking, Sven?"

He smiled. "Not a whole lot. What's shaking on your end?"

"The usual." She winked at him as if they shared a great secret. "How're things going with amore? How was dinner last night?"

"You'll have to use your psychic powers of divination, Alberta."

She shot him a gap-toothed grin and swatted at him with a tattered-lace folding fan. "Don't get all sassy-mouthed with me. I detect a note of frustration and that's not psychic divination, that's deduction." Her look was part sly triumph and part sympathy. "She's not an easy one, is she?"

"I told you she wasn't my type."

"How late did you stay up researching addictions and addictive behaviors last night?"

That stopped him in his tracks. Both parts of it— that she knew Juliette's secret and that she knew he had been reading online until the wee hours of the morning about the disease.

She patted his arm. "I know you thought I was a phony, but I've got the gift…actually, my third husband thought it was a curse. You were up pretty late, weren't you?"

"Yeah." He'd hung up the phone with his mom and found he simply couldn't leave it alone. He'd wanted to know more about what it was Juliette dealt with. He wasn't quite sure why and he didn't particularly feel the need to examine the why too carefully. He shrugged. "Information is knowledge and knowledge is power." He still wasn't sure he believed in psychic abilities, but Alberta seemed to have some hellaciously deductive reasoning skills. "Okay, any sage words of advice?"

"Slow and steady wins the race…and that's what she's going to require."

And on the off chance she did have some psychic abilities… "I guess I'm looking more for a psychic cheat sheet as to what's going on in her head."

"Ah, once again you're looking for the easy route and she's not going to be easy, Sven. But you knew that, didn't you?"

That was precisely why he'd stayed away for so long. And as to why he wasn't running like hell in the other direction now…well, he wasn't altogether sure.

"My mother is—"

"Worried," she finished for him. "I know. She loves you and quite frankly everything's always come fairly easy to you, hasn't it? You've led a pretty charmed life. Perhaps your mother's not as afraid of Juliette as she is of what might happen when your mettle is actually tested. And Juliette will test your mettle."

For about two seconds he considered taking offense, but the truth of the matter was he *had* led a somewhat charmed life. And was it his fault that things had come easy to him or for him?

"No, it's not your fault." God, it was just freaky and invasive when she answered the questions tumbling around in his head. "Are you up to the task?"

Sven didn't automatically answer. Was he? While he'd like to say yes, he really wasn't sure. Did he want to be? Or did he just want to walk away? Crazy as it seemed, even to him, walking away wasn't an option. Sorenson family legend held that they'd descended from Vikings—as if there was a Swedish family around who didn't want to claim a piece of that lore. But when you got past all the romantic claptrap, Vikings hadn't been particularly nice guys. They were ruthless invaders, men of steel who lived by the sword. Was that in him?

It was as if, standing in the middle of the sidewalk in Good Riddance with the May sun warming his shoulders, he could almost feel the forging of steel down his spine, through him, a resolve he'd never quite known before.

He held his head a tad higher and straighter. "I believe I am up to the task."

She looked pleased. "You know it's not just Juliette. Your parents may not support you."

He'd gotten a smidge of that last night on the phone with his mom. "Storming walls, scaling defenses, a relentless assault—sure, I've got it all in me."

Did he? Saying and doing were two different things. The truth was he'd sort of floated through life, no real responsibility. Sure, he had a job and he worked pretty steadily, but he liked not having to step up to any particular plate. Eric had always been the overachiever, whereas Sven had just drifted.

Something zinged into his mind that he'd totally forgotten about. He'd been two years behind Eric, who had set a very high bar. It was third grade parent-teacher conferences. He had Mrs. Marberry, the same third-grade teacher who'd taught Eric. Sven had been out on the playground but run back in to the bathroom. He'd overheard Mrs. Marberry telling his parents that they shouldn't expect as much out of Sven. She'd said he was a sweet boy and bright enough, but he didn't have Eric's potential. She'd suggested they not push him too hard, past his capabilities. Damn, he hadn't thought about that in years.

But now that he thought about it, he'd sort of taken that and run with it, sitting back and gliding through life. And Mom and Pops hadn't expected too much. Hell, he realized in a moment of insight, he hadn't expected too much from himself.

Why try hard if no one expected anything from you? Wasn't that why he'd avoided Juliette from the beginning, because she was too much trouble? Maybe it wasn't the trouble aspect at all but more that he might fail. That she would be a challenge had been apparent from the get-go. But there was something about her, something that made him want to dig deep, to not just walk away.

Alberta tapped her head with her fan. "You do, you know."

He hoped like hell so. "Well, let's get a move on. I've got my work cut out for me."

"That you do, my boy, that you do. But I have faith in you."

He and Alberta—an army of two.

He hoped it was enough.

6

"Okay, that's a wrap," Tessa said, ending the rehearsal.

Juliette's attention had only been half on the task at hand, much as it had been all day.

"Enjoy the weekend and I'll see everyone on Monday," Tessa added. Rehearsals were limited to Monday through Friday evenings.

Tucking her notes and clipboard beneath her arm, Juliette didn't let any grass grow under her feet. She beelined for the exit. All evening she'd made sure there was someone else around as she and Sven worked on the set. She'd felt him looking at her, watching her—not in some creepy way. It had been kind of nice except it was distracting.

Once their eyes had met and held across the stage. Heat had stolen through her as if his fingers were actually sliding over her skin in a gossamer caress.

Her breath had quickened, her pulse pounded, heart raced…and her brain had issued a loud, resounding *no*. Fight or flight? She wasn't sure how much fight she had in her to combat the attraction she felt for him, so flight was the only viable option. Plus, she specialized in flight.

She hurried down the stairs, welcoming the slight breeze against her heated cheeks. She'd almost reached her truck when boots sounded on the stairs behind her and the wind carried Sven's scent.

"Wait up, boss," he called out.

In spite of her need to escape, his "boss" fool-ishness coaxed a smile out of her. Her hand on the side panel of the truck, she paused, turning to him. "Yes?"

He sauntered over, his tool belt hanging low on his hips. Okay, she was losing it because she found it incredibly sexy. A tool belt. She'd definitely taken leave of good sense.

He stopped, once again, backlit by the sun, look-ing like some tool-belted, larger-than-life Norse hero. "I was hoping you could help me out."

She doubted it. "What do you need?"

The husky rasp of her voice gave it an altogether different meaning. For a moment she glimpsed something slightly wicked and hot in his blue eyes.

The air between them seemed to sizzle. She looked away first. Over his shoulder, Ellie waved goodbye. Juliette absently returned the wave.

Sven shifted, as if determined to catch and hold her attention. "I ordered dinner to go from Gus's."

She didn't see what this had to do with her at all. A part of her brain registered that he was, quite possibly, the most handsome man she'd ever met. And once again, that had nothing to do with the matter at hand, even though she didn't know exactly what the matter at hand was. "Okay..."

"They gave me two dinners."

"I see." Well, she didn't really, but he'd paused, so she had to say something. She trusted that momentarily his meaning would be as clear as the blue in his eyes.

"And then I had to drop my truck off at Donna's and it won't be ready until tomorrow afternoon, so I don't have a ride home." He looked at her expectantly.

"What about Skye and Dalton?" She didn't care if she sounded slightly desperate. She was. It was too nice, too comfortable, too cozy at Shadow Lake with Sven.

"It didn't work out. So, what do you say? Could you give me a lift?" She supposed she could drop him at the road. "And help me out with the extra meal?" So much for dropping him at the road.

She hesitated, wanting to say yes, not wanting to say yes. God, the man turned her into a mess.

"Just for the record, this is not a date. Not remotely a date." Why was she smiling? Why was her resolve to stay away from him crumbling second by second? "See, if it was a date I would be show-ered—" she would not think about him naked in the shower "—and would've changed clothes, so it's not a date. This is a favor. You'd definitely be doing me a favor, helping me out."

He was fun and somewhere along the way she'd forgotten how to have fun. She wasn't sure if she'd ever actually known how.

She grasped at one last straw. "Petey?" Petey lived out past Shadow Lake.

Sven shook his head, his hair brushing against his shoulders. "I tried. He's got a date with Donna to-night. He's going to help her with an engine—mine. See, that's a date. Look, don't take this the wrong way or anything, but you're my last resort. I really hated to ask you because I was afraid of this very thing, that you might misconstrue my intentions, and I know how you feel about the date thing. I suppose if you've got something else going on I can walk."

She couldn't help laughing at his foolishness.

He grinned. "It's only about six…maybe seven miles. It won't get dark for another couple of hours or so."

It was all so ridiculously over the top, how could she not say yes? And how was it that she seemed to-tally susceptible to this particular man's charm? The more pertinent question would be who could possi-bly be immune to his foolishness?

She shook her head in resignation and exaspera-tion. And somewhere inside her, no small measure of excitement and anticipation blossomed unbidden, like a rainbow appearing at the end of a storm. "Just get in."

He rounded the front of the truck to the passen-ger side. "Thanks. And for the record, if we were on a date…" He trailed off as he opened the door and climbed in.

She settled in the driver's seat. "I'm going to regret asking, but what? Finish it." She fit the key in the ignition, turning it over.

"I like my women in dresses."

Really? He was totally incorrigible…and irresist-ible. "Then today is your lucky day that we don't have a date, because not only am I not one of your women—" the very notion tightened her entire body "—I don't own a dress." She headed north.

"For real? You really don't own a dress?" Ha. She'd got him. "Wait…yes, you do. You had on a dress one evening at Gus's. I saw you."

Actually, she had a closet full. She loved wear-ing dresses at home and she occasionally wore them into town. She liked soft loose flowing materials that were both feminine and comfortable. Some women liked frilly underwear, she liked dresses.

And she was sad and pathetic because the fact that he'd noticed made her want to smile all over… or run screaming in the other direction. And she'd never felt more alive and such a ridiculous sense of joy at teasing like this with him. She laughed. Again. "I had you going for a minute."

"Only a minute. Hey, don't forget to swing by Gus's." He waved her over.

"Why do I need to stop by Gus's?" Nonetheless, she pulled over.

"Dinner."

"You said they gave you two orders by mistake. How can that be if you hadn't picked them up yet? Riddle me that, Joker." And come to think of it, where were his take-out boxes? He had her so befuddled she couldn't think clearly half the time.

"Alberta." He didn't miss a beat. "She's psycho, you know."

"Psychic."

"Same difference. Anyway, she told me on the way to rehearsal Lucky was going to screw up and give me an extra meal. Who am I to argue with Alberta?"

Her earlier conversation with Logan came to mind. Yes, Logan was incredibly fortunate Sven hadn't been interested in Jenna because Jenna wouldn't have stood a chance and Logan would've been so knocked out of the running. In her book, other men paled in comparison to Sven.

SVEN WATCHED JULIETTE as she finished the last of her dinner from the plastic box on her lap. Once again they were on the front porch, enjoying the remnants of sunlight across the lake's surface. Her profile was etched in relief—her straight nose, the ridge of her cheekbones, the pout of her lips, the curve of her eyelashes.

"You have an interesting face," he said.

Rain began to fall, pinging against the roof. "How's that?"

"It's the angles and curves." As if someone had opened a water faucet, the random drops became a downpour. The curtain of water veiled them in privacy, further isolating them from the rest of the world. There was a feeling of rightness to it.

"Guess it's just as well that you didn't leave me to walk home," Sven said, eyeing the onslaught.

"What? Do you think you'd have melted?"

She was actually teasing him. He liked it.

"There's one way to know." He stepped off the porch into the downpour, spreading his arms and facing the sky. Within seconds he was soaked. Despite being heavy and steady, it wasn't a driving, stinging rain.

"Sven!"

"You're right." He grinned at her through the downpour. "I'm not melting."

She walked to the edge of the porch, laughing. He loved making her laugh—it made him feel good all the way through.

"You're crazy." There was amusement, wonderment and maybe a tinge of wistfulness in her tone.

"Well, I am wet, maybe a little crazy, but definitely not melting." He took a step toward the porch. "Wonder if you'd pass the test?"

Her eyes widened. "Don't even—"

He advanced. "What? Scared of a little rain?"

She retreated. "You wouldn't—"

"Dare?" He kept coming. She had no idea how much he was willing to dare. "Oh, Ms. Miller, yes, I would."

She was still laughing and protesting and shaking her head when he gained the porch. "No."

He scooped her up and paused. She was warm and dry and oh so right against him. Then he carried her down the stairs out into the deluge.

"Sven!" She was laughing, delight and outrage and something indefinable dancing across her face. He stood, holding her, her hip pressed against his groin, her head at his shoulder, as the water washed over both of them.

He set her on her feet, the water plastering her hair against her head, molding her clothes to her curves. He didn't, couldn't release her. She felt too right in his arms. Mascara streaked her cheeks. "I'll be damned," he said. "You *are* melting."

He reached down and swiped the dark streak from her pale skin. In that instant, the laughter died between them. He was certain he'd never seen a woman more hauntingly, achingly beautiful than the one standing before him with her once again too-serious brown eyes and bedraggled hair.

His finger against her skin, he cupped her cheek in his palm. "You are so beautiful."

"You're crazy." But this time the words were spoken softly, as if he couldn't possibly think her beautiful standing in the pouring rain.

"You do seem to have that impact on me," he said.

He wrapped his other arm around her and kissed her. It was a melding of skin and water and warmth in the spring rain. She wound her arms about his neck. The last vestige of sanity deserted him with the stroke of her tongue against his and the press of her breasts against his chest. Her nipples stabbed against him through their clothes. Desire thickened his cock.

He wanted to strip her naked and feel the slide of her bare skin against his. He wanted to take her turgid points into his mouth, fill his hands with her bare bottom and ease into her slick channel as the rain fell over them.

It was as if he couldn't get enough of her. He was no longer content with just knowing the taste of her lips and the feel of her tongue. He kissed the side of her jaw and moved to the tender wet flesh of her neck. Her sigh seemed to float above the ping of the rain against the roof. He licked the rivulet of water along her collarbone.

He molded his hands against the curve of her back, feeling the dip of her spine against his fingertips as if she were pliable clay taking form beneath his touch.

He captured her nipple in his mouth, suckling her through the cloth and she curled her fingers into his shoulders. And then she pushed ever so slightly away with her palms and he immediately released her.

She stumbled to the porch and up the stairs, wrapping her hands around the post, as if seeking its support. He joined her.

The water molded her hair to her scalp and her clothes to her curves. Her nipples were outlined against her wet shirt. Much as he longed to scoop her up again and carry her inside to peel away her wet garments and lay her naked on his sheets, he felt her wariness.

The steady rain, punctuated by their uneven breathing, filled the space around them. Water puddled beneath them. He could at least dry her off.

"I'll be right back," Sven said, moving toward the door.

"I need to leave."

"Hold on."

He hurried into the cabin and grabbed the other clean towel from the bathroom—he only had two since it was just him—and returned to the porch.

As if carved in stone, Juliette hadn't moved. She reached for the towel. Ignoring her outstretched hand, he plied the cotton over her hair. She stood stock-still, her eyes wary, her expression guarded as he dried her face and neck.

He wasn't sure what surprised him more—his compulsion to do this or that she allowed it. He moved behind her, blotting the back of her neck. Finally, he draped the bath sheet about her shoulders.

He wrapped his arm around her waist, pulling her to rest against his chest and hips. He pressed a kiss to the side of her neck. For a second she leaned back into him.

"Juliette," he spoke impulsively, from the heart. "I don't want you to go tonight. Stay, please."

She shook her head, stepping away and out of his arms. He could've kicked himself for speaking without thinking first, for pushing too hard too fast.

"I can't. I'm not... No." She wrapped her arms about her, grasping the towel's edges, pulling it tighter.

"I understand. It's okay. I'm sorry I...I shouldn't have asked." He felt uncharacteristically tongue-tied and gauche.

"Don't." She turned and rested her fingers against his lips. "Please don't apologize." She dropped her hand to her side. "I should go." She placed the towel over the back of the chair.

"I know." He didn't want her to leave and he crazily, desperately didn't want her to leave without knowing he would see her again before Monday's rehearsal. "I'm going to pick out a puppy tomorrow afternoon. My dog I'd had for ten years, Susie, died last summer. I'm finally ready for another dog. Will you come with me? I'm going out to Marsha Monroe's to pick one. She's got a litter of ten. I could use some help. Please."

The rain ended as quickly as it had begun.

"But it's your dog, your puppy. I don't know why...."

He didn't know why, either. "Neither do I, really, but I want you there."

She stood silently for what seemed like forever. Finally she spoke. "What time?"

Yes! "Around two. I could swing by and pick you up about one forty-five."

Another long pause and he found he was holding his breath.

"Okay," she said, stepping off the porch.

"Drive safely going home tonight."

"Of course." She looked at him as if he'd truly lost it. He was pretty sure he had. "This is Good Riddance."

The gravel crunched beneath their feet as he walked her to her truck. "You just never know. Look, call my cell phone now. That way you have my number and I have yours. Then drop me a text when you get home."

"That's not necessary." She opened her door. "I've been getting home on my own for a long time."

"I'd sleep better." He'd never felt this protectiveness before. There was something about her that seemed to call to something inside him; that made him want to put himself between her and the rest of the world. She wasn't weak and she wasn't clingy, but it was as if he felt needed for the first time ever, which was damn strange considering she hadn't even remotely hinted at needing him. If anything, she'd given off exactly the opposite vibe.

She climbed in. "I assure you, you'll sleep just fine regardless." She closed the door, ending the conversation. Almost.

"Yes, boss," he said.

Sven had a feeling sleep would be a long time in coming tonight.

JULIETTE PILED HER WET clothes in the bathtub—she'd deal with them later—and belted the terry-cloth robe around her waist. From the kitchen, her kettle whistled. She padded into the other room and poured boiling water over a tea bag.

A warm cup of ginger-peach green tea, decaf, was just what she needed. Setting the timer for four minutes, she picked up the phone.

She could also use an ear and a word of advice to help her sort through things. The sounds of the various wind chimes drifting through her open kitchen window failed to soothe her as they usually did.

None of it brought any relief from the restless

longing inside her. The dampness between her thighs had nothing to do with the pouring rain. Her body clamored for Sven's touch, for the hot wet of his mouth on her breast, the gust of his breath against her skin. It was as if her sexuality, long dormant, had roared to life with a vengeance with his touch.

It was disconcerting. Inconvenient. Frighteningly exhilarating. She felt almost drunk from their encounter and she hadn't had a drop.

She touched Sue's name on her phone's screen, setting it to speaker phone.

"Hey, chickie, what's up?" Sue's voice filled the kitchen. "I haven't heard from you in a while. You okay?"

In her late fifties, Sue was more than a friend. She was the one person who knew Juliette as thoroughly as anyone could or, perhaps, ever would. Sue was her sponsor, the woman who'd spent a year helping Juliette work through the 12-step program of Alcoholics Anonymous.

In the early days, and occasionally in the subsequent years, when the temptation, the craving to drink had gnawed at Juliette, Sue had been there to talk her through it. Sometimes it was one day at a time, one hour at a time. When things were really bad, Juliette had taken it minute by minute. And while she didn't feel the need to drink now, she did feel the need to talk to someone who knew all the nuances of her past.

"I'm fine. I haven't had a drink and I don't want one."

"That's some good news. So, tell me what's going on."

Juliette pulled out the tea bag and gave Sue the rundown on Sven, leaving none of it out.

"Good. It's about time."

"What?" Mug in hand, Juliette retreated to her bedroom. She settled back against the lace-ruffled pillow.

"You heard me. You can bury yourself in that little town, but sooner or later you've got to live."

"But—"

"There's a difference between being sober, which you have been, and being sober and living, and I'm not sure how much living you've been doing. You've got a good solid foundation under you, Juliette. Trust yourself."

"I do, but—"

"Maybe you trust yourself, but you've got to move past the fear. Let me guess, this is the first time you've ever kissed someone when you were totally sober, without a glass of wine or two to loosen up."

Juliette rested her forehead in her hand, her eyes closed, willing herself not to go back to all those other times, not to dredge up the past. "Yes."

"And I'm guessing this was better than all those other times combined?"

Better didn't begin to describe it. She *ached* for him. "Yes."

"It's time, Juliette, to live sober—to kiss a man, to make love, to laugh, to embrace in the rain. Open yourself to life's experiences."

"I don't want to fail at another relationship." Old feelings of inadequacy surfaced and rolled through her.

"You won't. Good Lord, don't you know most men are scared to death that a woman wants to put a ring on their finger? Enjoy what's coming your way. You're attracted to him, right?"

She resisted the urge to laugh hysterically. "You could safely say that."

"He's a decent guy?"

"He's actually very nice. Almost too nice. He comes from this really great family, he's smart and funny and good-looking and talented." And if he truly understood how flawed she was, he'd leave her alone. Although she'd tried to tell him…

"Oh, I see." And Juliette was fairly certain Sue did see. "He's too good, isn't he? You deserve good things, hon." Sue did know her. She understood exactly what was going through Juliette's head.

"Trust that the things that are meant to come to you will come to you."

"So, you think I should go tomorrow?"

"Yes, I think you should go tomorrow." Juliette could hear the smile in Sue's voice. "And I think you should wear a dress when you're ready to wear a dress. Then, when you're ready, I think you should stay the night."

"You do?"

"I do."

Was she ready for a date? Did she want a lover?

Her body screamed yes, but her mind wasn't quite convinced.

7

SVEN'S HEART WAS THUMPING in his chest like crazy as he drove down the potholed road to Juliette's place. She rented the place. He spotted her truck and made the left onto the driveway, which was in even worse shape than the road.

The first thing he noticed, considering it would be impossible to miss, was the assortment of wind chimes, whirligigs and weather vanes scattered throughout the clearing that served as a yard. He parked behind her Land Rover and made his way toward the door. It was a little busier than he preferred, but some of her stuff was pretty cool.

Sven took his time, strolling through the assortment. Tibetan prayer flags, strung across the front of a year-round porch, fluttered in the breeze. It should have been a cacophony as the various materials— glass pieces, silverware, wood, copper tubing—produced their own sound. It wasn't. It all combined and worked to produce a sound that was both soothing and energizing.

Before he reached the pathway to the porch door, it opened and Juliette stepped out onto the covered landing. He did a double take, a slow smile spreading across his face. He'd been uptight all morning, but suddenly all was incredibly right with his world.

Just for the record, if it was a date...I like my women in dresses.

She was wearing a dress.

A short-sleeved dress in graduated shades of pink and cream followed the curve of her hip, ending in three ruffled flounces at the hem that hit her a couple of inches above the knee. She had nice legs. Very, very nice legs.

"Hi." She nodded toward his truck. "How's it running?"

"Great. Donna's a genius with engines." *Especially when there wasn't anything wrong with it.* He'd just wanted a reason to get Juliette to have dinner with him again. All was fair in love and war and this qualified as a bit of both.

"You look really, really nice. Great, in fact. It's a good look for puppy-picking."

A light blush stole up her neck and colored her cheeks. She really was beautiful—soft and feminine but strong. Her short hair curled against her neck and cheek while her skin glowed fresh. She wore minimal makeup. He wished he'd brought her flowers. He should've brought flowers. Next time.

He stepped closer and reached out to touch her earrings, his finger brushing the soft curve of her cheek and the delicate shell of her ear. "Beautiful."

The puppies could wait. Everything could wait. He wanted nothing more than to touch her, to know the hidden secrets of her body, the curves beneath the dress, the texture of her skin, the expression on her face when he gave her pleasure. He dialed himself back. Last night he had moved too quickly. He dropped his hand to his side.

She tucked her hair behind her ear, even though it was already there. "They're origami cranes," she said.

"Did you make them?"

"No. I ordered them on the internet."

He glanced around the yard. "I take it you like wind art."

She smiled, the curve of her lips, her scent, touching him deep inside, like a lover's caress. "You think? What gave it away?"

"So, do you internet shop this, as well?" He made a sweeping gesture with his hand to encompass her collection.

"I make the wind chimes. It's a hobby." There was a shy edge to her smile. "Sometimes it's almost an obsession." She laughed self-consciously.

"How'd you get interested in that?"

She shrugged. "There's just something about the air. And it's as if the chimes…the whirligigs…the flags…it's a tangible manifestation of something you can't actually see because we don't actually see the wind. It's like looking at freedom."

"You said once before that flying was freedom."

"It is. It's like nothing else. I'd rather be up in the air than anywhere else. Don't we need to go? You said Marsha's expecting you at two?"

"Yeah, you're right. We should roll out or we're going to be late." She stepped off the landing and he placed his hand lightly in the small of her back. "I'm glad you're going with me."

"I think I am, too." Her quiet smile felt like a caress.

They walked to his truck and he opened her door, earning him a look. "Uh, thanks."

"You're welcome."

He climbed into the cab. She smelled good, fresh. He tightened his grip on the steering wheel rather than reach for her and pull her into his arms. He backed out the driveway and they bounced down the road, a comfortable silence between them. When they turned out onto the main road leading to Marsha's and picked up speed, the wind blowing through the open windows increased. "If that's too much air or you're worried about your hair, we can roll the windows up some."

Juliette laughed. "I told you, I love the wind and my hair just kind of does its own thing."

"I like it. It suits you."

"Thanks. I'm not a high-maintenance woman by any stretch of the imagination."

She might not be high-maintenance but she was by far the most complicated, complex woman he'd ever met. That, however, he kept to himself.

He glanced over at her. Her hair seemed to dance about her head, buffeted by the airflow. "I like the way the wind's whipping through your hair."

She laughed. "Are you making fun of me?"

"No. Not at all. I do like it. It's cool."

She turned a bit in the seat, canting one of her shapely legs toward him. "So, I'm not much of a dog person. What are you looking for in a puppy? General cuteness? Male? Female? Do you want it to be a working dog or just a pet?"

"More of a companion. I've never had a real need for a working dog. Susie went with me everywhere. She was smart as a whip."

"What happened to her?"

"Old age. One morning she couldn't get up and then she looked at me and I knew."

She reached over and touched his arm lightly, resting her fingers briefly against his forearm in a gesture of comfort. "I'm sorry. It must have been hard."

He nodded. "It was one of the hardest things I've

ever had to do. Nah, it *was* the hardest thing." Which was why he'd had to give it some time and distance before he got another dog. "It doesn't really matter whether it's a male or a female."

"Then that should make it easy."

"Yeah?" Spoken like a true puppy-picking neophyte. "We'll see."

They pulled into Marsha's place and she was waiting outside. Marsha, who must've been somewhere in her mid-thirties, had had a rough year. First, her long-term girlfriend had packed up and moved back to wherever she was from in the lower forty-eight to take care of an ailing parent. Then a couple of months ago her younger sister, Teddy, who Marsha had raised after their mom died, had moved to New York. At least Marsha still had her dogs.

"Sven...Juliette." She greeted each of them with a firm handshake and a reserved smile. "So, you ready to see the little rascals?" She cut right to the chase, but then again, Marsha always seemed most at ease when she was talking about or was with her dogs.

"Sounds good."

"Hold on a sec, then. I kept them up until you got here. Pups running around and big trucks pulling in can be a bad combination. Plus, you never know with the eagles and hawks. That'd be bad."

About a month ago another breeder had lost a pup to an eagle. It didn't happen often, but still, Sven understood her caution. As if it had overheard the conversation, an eagle's call resounded in the distance.

Marsha crossed the expanse of green lawn that fronted the house and formed the side yard to the kennel. She opened the door, whistled and puppies literally tumbled out. Yipping and yapping, they tripped over their short stocky legs and each other in their haste. It was an array of damn cute pups.

Sven glanced at Juliette. She watched the puppies, a smile wreathing her face, as the little ones scampered across the lawn toward them. And this was a woman who professed she didn't much care for dogs? Okay, then.

She sank to her knees and they rushed her, jockeying for attention. Sven squatted beside her. Laughing, her hands entangled in puppiedom, she glanced over at him, unguarded joy shining in her eyes. "Aren't they just so cute?"

His breath lodged in his throat. Sunlight dappled her face, picking out a couple of freckles on the bridge of her nose. She looked young and carefree and he realized, once he caught a glimpse of her without it, how guarded she usually was. The look in her eyes seared straight through to his soul.

And it was as if in that moment he found a temporary purpose he really hadn't known was lacking in his life. His short-term mission was to see more of that joy in her eyes. And it was totally self-serving, because it simply made him feel good inside.

THE RASP OF A WET TONGUE against her forearm tickled and Juliette laughed yet again. Had she ever laughed so much in her life as she had in the past few days? The sun warmed her head and shoulders. The puppies, soft fur balls of unbridled energy, raced between her and Sven. For such a big man, he was incredibly gentle with them. The irrational notion crossed her mind that he'd be great with kids.

A familiar feeling washed over her, but it was out of context. It took her a second to realize what she felt was the same sensation she experienced in the air, in her plane—free, safe, happy in the moment. She'd never, ever felt this way before on the ground. The sheer novelty of it broadened her smile and she relaxed into the moment of sunshine, puppies…and Sven.

"He's a bruiser," Sven said, picking up a gray male with a distinctive black mask who stood obviously bigger than the others.

Marsha smiled, sinking to her haunches next to Juliette. "That's exactly what I call him—Bruiser."

The puppies shifted their attention to Sven, who was holding one of their own. Juliette noticed for the first time a pup on the fringe of the melee. Smaller than the others, it hung back. As if it sensed her interest, it looked up. Juliette found herself looking into the softest, kindest eyes she'd ever encountered. It was like gazing into the eyes of a very old soul.

"Who is that?" she said to Marsha, pointing to the one hanging back from the rest.

"I call her Baby. As you can see, she's the runt of the litter. There's not always a runt, but Baby definitely qualifies."

Juliette held out her hand. Baby tentatively started toward her, only to be knocked out of the way by the rush of three others. Doggedly, no pun intended, Baby pushed through the group, nipping at one.

"Well, I'll be hanged with a new rope." Marsha rocked back on her heels. "I've never seen her do that. Usually she doesn't bother to take on the others. She just holds back and lets them have whatever."

Baby nudged Juliette's finger with a wet nose. "Can I pick her up?"

"Sure."

Juliette scooped up the little girl dog. She was soft, but not nearly as plump as the others. Feeling a little awkward and unsure, Juliette cuddled the pup to her. She could've sworn the dog sighed as she settled against Juliette's chest.

Sven grinned. "I didn't think you were a dog person."

She could've kicked him for that. It just wasn't something you said in front of a breeder. "You learn something new about yourself all the time, I guess."

Marsha looked from Sven to Juliette and then her gaze encompassed the both of them. "That's funny, well, ironic really. You've got Bruiser—" she nodded at Sven "—and you've got Baby—" this nod was directed at Juliette "—and the two of them have this kind of weird connection the rest don't seem to have. At chow time, Bruiser looks out for her, but then Baby gives back, because she licks him until he falls asleep. It's the funniest thing I've ever seen."

"Well," Sven said to Juliette. "So much for you helping me choose. It looks like today's a his 'n hers. One for you and one for me."

Automatically a protest rose to Juliette's lips and then she stopped, opening herself up to the possibility. Why not? As if sensing her indecision, Baby snuggled deeper against Juliette.

She was thirty-two. She'd never had a dog before. Heck, she'd never had any pet before. She wasn't particularly drawn to dogs or cats—or babies, for that matter, not that they were pets—but it was almost as if Baby wasn't a dog. She was more like… Juliette didn't know…just a being, a soul in a dog body, who obviously liked Juliette. And Juliette liked her. She seesawed in indecision.

"I never try to talk anyone into a dog," Marsha said. "It's a big responsibility and a big commitment. I love my dogs and I only want them going to a home where they're going to get the best care. But that said, it'd be nice if Bruiser and Baby could see one another once in a while because they're attached. You never know where the dogs will wind up—I've

got a buyer flying in tomorrow from River's Ford—
and if these two could stay close to one another...."

Juliette just didn't know. "It is a big decision. I
need to think about it."

"Sure. If you think you're not going to want her
though, could let me know before Joe gets here tomorrow? She's such a runt it's unlikely he'll want
her, but it's not really fair to take her out of the running, if you know what I mean."

Every fiber within her protested at the notion of
some faceless stranger named Joe hauling Baby off
to River's Ford. She didn't care how nice Joe might
be, he wouldn't feel about Baby the way Juliette did
right now.

She remembered Sven saying his dog had gone to
work with him. What would it be like to have Baby
up in the sky with her?

"How do you think she'd do in a plane?"

Marsha smiled. "There's only one way to find out.
But these dogs are laid-back and extremely adapt-
able. And she's a runt, not a scaredy-cat."

It felt right, kind of scary, but right. "I want her."

"And I'll take him."

"You might want to think on that. He's going to
require a little bit of work. He's a sweet dog but he's
not the brightest or sharpest of the lot. One of the
others would be easier. I'm just telling you because
it's got to be a good match and you've got to know

what you're getting into. Bruiser's going to be a challenge."

Sven hesitated, obviously thinking about it. Juliette wouldn't be surprised if he picked another puppy. He didn't strike her as the kind of guy who'd want a challenging puppy when the pick of the litter was available.

He looked down at Bruiser for a couple of long seconds and then he looked back up at Marsha, a slow smile curling his lips. "Sometimes the best things aren't the easiest. I want him."

Something inside Juliette turned over.

Marsha smiled at Sven. "Bruiser for you." She looked at Juliette. "Baby for you?"

Juliette glanced at Sven and he gave a slight nod of his head that was more encouragement than approval.

Rubbing her chin against the puppy's head, Juliette said, "Baby for me."

"All right then," Marsha said, rising to her feet. "I'll go inside and pull the paperwork together, and how about you pick them up the middle of next week?"

"Next week?" Juliette said. "She's not going with me today?" Now that she'd made up her mind, she was reluctant to let Baby go.

"Nope. They need about another week with their mom, plus a cooling-off period is always a good thing. It's easy to make a decision in the heat of the moment when they're crowding around you all cute, but if someone leaves and has buyer's remorse, I'd rather not have my dogs caught in the middle. I have a suggested list of items you'll need to take proper care of her." Marsha smiled. "But you can hold on to her while I go get that together."

Marsha headed for the front door. Juliette looked down. Baby was snoozing.

"Thanks a lot," Juliette said to Sven. "I just bought a dog and I only came along for the ride."

He grinned, totally unrepentant. "Probably the second-best decision you ever made."

He was baiting her. She'd bite. "Really? And what would be the first best decision I ever made?"

"Going on a date with me today."

The man should come with a warning. Her pulse quickened. "Is that a fact? Who said it's a date?"

"You're wearing a dress, aren't you?"

"Maybe it was the only clean thing in my closet."

"Maybe, but I'm thinking not."

"Kind of an unusual first date, wouldn't you say? Going to pick out a puppy."

"You're an unusual kind of woman, so it fits. And the day's not over, so who knows what's going to happen next."

The look in his eyes sent a shiver down her spine and heat through her. "Maybe I have plans later."

"You most assuredly do…" He leaned slightly, closing the gap between them until his warm breath gusted against her ear. "With me," he said softly, as if imparting a secret.

"That's rather arrogant." Her voice was husky.

"Would you have me any other way?"

Heaven help her but his low tone, the smolder in his blue eyes, sent a slick wet heat gathering between her thighs. He didn't even have to touch her.

"Who says I want you?" They both knew she did.

"You're not answering the question, Juliette."

"You're putting the cart before the horse. I'd have to decide *if* I wanted you before I decided *how* I wanted you."

And she could bluff all day, but they both knew the answer to that.

8

SVEN CHUCKLED TO HIMSELF at Juliette's longing glance back as they turned out of Marsha's place. *I'm not a dog person.* Yeah, right. She'd obviously just never met the right dog. "She'll be fine."

"But she was so sad."

Baby had whined when Juliette handed her back over to Marsha. Obviously it was mutual adoration. It had been sweet. "And Marsha will take really good care of her until you pick her up next week."

"I know you're right, it's just…" She trailed off, her expression somewhat disconsolate. And he had just the cure for that.

"Let's go shopping," Sven said. Women were always all about shopping, weren't they?

"We both just got puppies. Aren't you shopped out? Plus, I spent money I hadn't planned to spend."

"I'll pay for Baby since I dragged you along. I'm sure Marsha will discount her since she's a runt."

Oh, hell. He'd just said the wrong thing. Ire flashed all over her face before she even opened her mouth.

"Absolutely not. I can pay for my own dog. I pay my own way. And Baby is worth just as much as Bruiser or any of the others." She stabbed a finger in his direction. "In fact, she's special." She crossed her arms over her chest and settled back in her seat, shooting him a look. "I should even pay a little extra for her, but she's definitely not discounted goods. Got it?"

Damn right he got it. There was certainly no mistaking where she was coming from. And it certainly was a change from that cool distance she maintained most of the time. She was like a tigress protecting a maligned cub. He was hard pressed not to laugh, but while he might not have had enough sense not to say what he did, he had enough sense not to laugh right now—she was just so damn cute. However, she was also serious as a heart attack and wouldn't find his amusement amusing in the least. He backpedaled for all he was worth. "All right, already. You're right and I'm sorry I went there."

She tilted her nose up in the air and speared him with a narrow-eyed glance. "Don't patronize me."

Done. He couldn't help it. He laughed, which earned him yet another glare. "I'm not. I swear I'm not patronizing you. I'm agreeing. You *are* right. Chill. Now, do you want to pull out that list Marsha

sent with you and do some internet shopping?"
Sweet Jesus, the woman was prickly as a hedgehog,
but she had been pretty torn up over leaving Baby, he
supposed. Bruiser had been easy. He'd licked Sven
once and then torn off across the yard.

He could almost feel her mentally waffling and
then she relaxed, her energy changed. "Okay."

"My place okay? I was thinking we could maybe
have a picnic somewhere along the lake, if you're up
for a walk."

She paused. Did she have to weigh everything?
Apparently she did. After a few seconds she nodded.
"That sounds good."

"I actually cleaned up the cabin."

She laughed. "I guess that sounds good, too. I
suppose I'll know after I see it."

"Maybe I should just bring my laptop outside to
the porch."

"What? Are you afraid I'll discover your secrets
if I go inside?"

Her tone was teasing, but he thought it was an interesting choice of words on her part. "I don't have
any secrets, although I will confess to some bad
habits."

"Name one."

That was easy. It drove his mother bat-shit crazy
and had annoyed the heck out of his girlfriend from
a couple of years ago. "I squeeze the toothpaste from
the middle. Always have."

"Ooooh. That's pretty bad right there."

She really wanted to know? "I've been known to go out in a chatroom or two." Alaska was a big state and he'd moved around a lot with his work, so he didn't always have a steady girlfriend. And sometimes there weren't any eligible women to be found. However, he never "chatted" when he was involved with someone. He figured he didn't want his girl doing that to him, so he'd play straight with her, as well.

"Webcam sex?"

"Not webcam, but…" No pictures, but instant messaging could get…intense.

"Yeah, I got you." She shrugged. "I don't think you're in the minority there."

"What about you? Your secrets? Bad habits?" Her expression shifted the moment the words left his mouth. Guarded didn't begin to describe her.

"I think we've pretty much covered it—the alcohol and two ex-husbands."

Hadn't she warned him she came with enough baggage to fill her cargo space? No lie. "Can we just forget about those for a while?"

"But they're a part of who I am."

Surely she didn't think an addiction and two husbands defined her. "They're part of your past… There's a whole lot more to you than that. Focus on the other part, let me get to know the rest of you."

"Why?"

"I don't know. I really don't know. All I know is that I can't stop thinking about you, about that kiss."

"Does that line work every time?"

He was fairly certain she was trying to offend him, put him off. He wasn't offended. "I don't know. I guess we're both about to find out, since this is the first time I've ever used it."

She turned her head away from him to look out the window. "I don't want to be part of a game."

Neither did he. Beneath her shell, he sensed a chasm of vulnerability. He didn't want to hurt her. And dammit, he didn't want to be hurt. Did he only want her because he didn't think he could have her? Was it the challenge of figuring her out? Unlocking her puzzle? Scaling her fortress? He didn't think so, but then again, Alberta had been correct. He'd never had to work very hard at getting what he wanted, be it a job, woman or pretty much anything else. There was something about her that made him want to be a better man, to dig within himself.

However, he could honestly say to her, "I'm not into games, Juliette. I play poker some with the guys up at Gus's, but other than that…"

She looked at him once again. "Neither am I. So, we'll just let things unfold, one day at a time, knowing that neither of us is looking for anything long-term or serious."

He honestly didn't know what he wanted outside of that he wanted her. He'd wanted her from the first time he'd kissed her so he wasn't so sure that short-term was going to be enough. And now wasn't the time to go there. He wasn't a gamer, but he was an occasional gambler. He could either fold or bluff. He bluffed. "Okay."

They pulled into the parking lot by Shadow Lake and he turned the truck off. They got out and en route he stopped her, catching her by the shoulder. "Wait a second. I've wanted to do this from the second you walked out on your porch today."

He kissed her, telling her without words how beautiful he found her, how glad he was with her here and now.

A slow smile tilted her just-kissed lips when he pulled away. "You wanted to do that all day?"

That…and more. He caught her hand in his. "I have."

Her fingers curled around his palm. "I wanted you to all day."

Her touch and her words pleased him. "You know, if you ever feel the urge for a kiss, feel free. I'm open to that."

She laughed. "Uh-huh. I bet you are."

He laughed. He could spend all day kissing her, but first things first. "The supply list from Marsha, woman. The list."

He opened the cabin door and she preceded him in. "We really can take the laptop outside if you'd rather," he said. The cabin was fine, but it was a poor substitute for the fresh air and the great outdoors.

"It is nice out there."

"And you can see the sky."

"That sounds good," she said. Her hand still in his, she smiled happily and his chest tightened.

He'd played poker before, but never had the stakes been this high or meant this much.

"WHAT DO YOU THINK?" Juliette tilted the screen to show Sven the aviator dog jacket she'd found. "I think yes."

"I think Baby has to have it." He grinned and there was an indulgence in his expression that set her heart fluttering. Make that fluttering more than it already was. She'd been achingly conscious of his sheer masculinity—his scent, the fall of his hair, the breadth of his shoulders, the tug of his jeans across his thighs and crotch—she was fluttering with all kinds of sexual energy for the man sharing the porch and computer screen with her.

Juliette clicked the order button and then paid for it. "Okay, done."

"Is that done for that item or done as in *done?*"

"Done-done." She realized she was quite hungry and it wasn't limited to her craving for him. "Not to be indelicate, but you were planning to feed me, weren't you?"

"That's the plan. The catch is you have to help.

Nothing gourmet. I thought we'd take sandwiches. Ham and cheese work for you?"

"Sure. You know it's time to eat when the dog treats you're ordering sound good."

Sven laughed and pushed off his chair. "Definitely. Come on, woman. I won't have you saying I starved you on our first date."

She handed him the laptop. "Ah, I get it. You're just protecting your reputation."

He opened the door, waiting on her to precede him into the room. "A man's got to do what a man's got to do."

Forty minutes later Sven stopped at a small clearing off the edge of the lake. "How's this strike you as a picnic spot?"

It was farther than they'd hiked the other night. She couldn't see either the cabins or Skye and Dalton's house. The lake stretched before them, backed by the mountains, all of it under a canvas of blue skies punctuated by layers of wispy clouds. A stand of fireweed bloomed between the clearing and the line of spruce beyond. It was so beautiful it nearly made her heart ache. "I'd say perfect."

"This is the place then, because it doesn't get better than perfect, does it?" He shrugged off the backpack he'd carried and pulled out a folded sheet.

"Do you ever run into Skye and Dalton?" she said.

"Not a lot. They keep to themselves at home.

They sometimes hike around the lake, but, as you know, Dalton's on flight standby today and Skye's still leery of getting out in what she calls 'the wilds' on her own."

She looked out over the lake. There was a soothing, peaceful quality to this spot. "It's a nice place to live."

"Yeah, it is."

While he spread the sheet, she unpacked the food. Ham and cheese on whole wheat, dill pickles, chocolate-chip cookies, potato chips and a thermos of water. She encountered something else in the bottom of the backpack. She pulled out a sketchbook and a box of pencils. "Did you mean to bring this?"

"I thought I might do some sketching if you wouldn't be bored."

"Not in the least. It's a beautiful spot. I can see why it would inspire you."

"Maybe it's not the setting that inspires me," he said, touching the tip of her nose and setting her heart clanging against her ribs. Good grief, that had to be one of the nicest things anyone had ever said to her. "Let's eat. I'm starving and you were hungry an hour ago."

They sat, mere inches separating them. Juliette bit into her sandwich and chased it with a bite of pickle. "Mmm," she said, "this is good."

"Yeah, it is."

It was just one of those times that didn't call for

conversation. She sat quietly munching away, finishing off her lunch in record time. It was nice simply *being* with him. She'd never felt this in anyone else's presence. Actually, it was sublime. He passed the cookies. "Dessert?"

"Sure." They looked homemade. "Did you make these?" She'd be impressed.

"Me? No. I haven't found a Crock-Pot cookie recipe yet." She giggled at his silly joke. "Jenna. She's practicing. She says every mom needs to be able to bake cookies."

It sounded like Jenna rationale. Her baby, who wasn't even here, wouldn't be gumming chocolate-chip cookies for some time, yet she was already practicing her baking. Juliette plucked one out of the container and bit into it…well, tried to bite into it. There was crisp and crunchy—and then there was bricklike. Juliette tried holding it in her mouth for a moment. Sure enough, it softened and she was able to bite off a piece. She chewed and swallowed, only because spitting just seemed tacky. It qualified as the worst thing she'd ever tasted. "That's awful. I'm not much of a cook, but I think she got too much baking soda in there." Jenna was so nice, Juliette felt bad for dissing her cookies. Aiming for a positive slant, she tacked on, "But they do look good."

"I guess it's just as well she's started practicing now," Sven said, putting the lid back on the container. So, she'd been the guinea pig.

"Poor Logan," she mused.

"Poor kid. Jenna'll be the room mom they all beg *not* to bring in cupcakes for the class."

Juliette laughed, but gigged him in the side with her elbow. "Don't be mean."

"Hey, Jenna knows she's a lousy cook, but all of a sudden she's equating it with some state of being a great mother. Maybe her hormones will level off when the baby pops out. Or maybe Logan can talk some sense into her. She was talking about making her own baby food the other day." He pointed toward the cookies. "Can you imagine?"

"No." She really couldn't. Wow, she was feeling so relaxed. The sun, the lap of the water, the drone of insects, the lull of gentle laughter, her tummy was full... She could hardly keep her eyes open.

Sven reached over and smoothed his hand over her head, his touch light. "It's okay if you want to nap. I wanted to sketch anyway."

It was a little disconcerting how easily he seemed to read her—but she'd think about it later. Now she really did just want to stretch out and close her eyes. "You really don't care? It seems sort of insulting on a date." She was only kind of kidding.

"I think we're both past all the rules, don't you? And I promise not to tell if you don't."

"Deal."

She stretched out on her back, angling her left arm over her eyes. The sun warmed her. She sank into a drowsy state, not quite asleep. She was too aware of her surroundings to truly slumber; she drifted into that place where she heard the rustle of paper, the rhythmic water against the shore, but she wasn't quite conscious. It was a dreamlike state where reality took on different forms, lines blurred and situations shifted fluidly without rhyme or reason. And there was always the sense of Sven's presence, as if he were standing sentinel, keeping a watchful eye on her behalf.

His touch, as light as a butterfly, fluttered over her arm, rousing her. She opened her eyes, her lids heavy. He was stretched beside her, propped on one arm, his blue eyes smiling at her. Instinctively, she smiled back.

He leaned forward and pressed small, tender kisses against her hairline. Lazily she reached up and linked her arm around his neck, inviting his lips to find hers. The dreamy thought floated through her mind that this must be what Sleeping Beauty had felt like when she finally awoke.

One kiss turned into many. She felt lush, brimming with the desire Sven stirred in her. He stroked her shoulder, her arm, the curve of her hip, her thigh where her dress had ridden up, each touch giving more than it took.

Meanwhile, she explored the breadth of his muscled shoulder, the ridges of his arms, the expanse of his back. It was unhurried, languid...delicious.

She'd always been uptight, unsure of herself, and she'd counted on alcohol to loosen her up, to give her an edge of bravado, to make her sexier. But it was amazing how relaxed she was now, how sure she was of her own sensuality with his hand on her thigh, and how satisfying it was to kiss, to touch and be touched, all stone-cold sober. The chemistry between them was more potent than any drink she'd ever downed.

Pulling him on top of her, she ran her fingers through his hair and welcomed his weight against her, the press of his obvious arousal between her thighs.

She tugged his shirt free of his jeans and up. He stopped kissing her long enough to tug it over his head and toss it aside. Oh. My. God. She pushed at him and he looked startled. She realized he was confused and thought she was rejecting him, asking him to stop.

"I just want to look at you," she said, not bothering to mask the husky awe in her voice. He sat back some, smiling, and Juliette knew precisely what she wanted. A boldness she didn't know she possessed sober rose within her. "All of you."

He stood, like a Norse god—big, blond and stunningly beautiful. While he unbuckled his belt, she reached for the hem of her dress, tugging it up and off, leaving only her bra and panties. The breeze and sun kissed her thighs, her belly and the tops of her breasts while his gaze scorched along the same path.

She leaned back on her elbows and looked up at him, the expression in his eyes gratifying, the smile on his face arousing. She was no innocent. She'd done things…slept with men…made some bad decisions… And been lucky there hadn't been more serious repercussions from her poor, or total lack of, judgment when she was drunk, none of which she was proud of. However, she realized in that moment of intense arousal that hovered between them like the dragonfly skimming over the water's surface, her sexuality was a healthy part of a sober her.

Sven bent down, unlacing his boots. Boots and socks gone, he unzipped his jeans, slid them down his hips and thighs, and stepped out of them. He hooked his fingers in the waistband of his boxer briefs and pulled them off in one smooth motion and step. He straightened, standing tall and proud and Juliette felt nearly dizzy from the rush he evoked inside her.

A cerulean sky framed his sun-kissed gold hair and broad, heavily muscled shoulders. He was a man who worked hard for a living. Darker blond hair furred his chest and arrowed down over a taut belly. His penis jutted from a thatch of light brown hair, while his scrotum hung heavy between his thighs. A thrill of anticipation and excitement, mixed with a twinge of trepidation, coursed through her. Maybe it had been the dream, perhaps it was the water and sky and trees, but for one crazy moment she felt as if he was her Viking warrior come to claim her as his own.

She silently laughed at herself. She could come up with this fanciful stuff and she wasn't even drinking.

She had no idea if it had been seconds, minutes or hours—time seemed to have lost its continuum—but Sven finally broke the silence. "You are exquisite."

She wasn't used to comments like that. It left her at a loss, so she simply laid back and opened her arms in supplication.

He came to her. He kissed her neck, the juncture where her neck met her shoulder, the curve of her arm, the bare skin between her bra and panties. The rasp of his faint beard was a delicious scrape against her.

She reached between them, tangling her fingers in the hair on his chest, fingering the points of his nipples, finding her way down his big body until her hand encountered the rigid length of his cock. He was warm, veined satin in her hand, against her fingers. He trembled beneath her touch and she felt both powerful and humble that she was here with this man at this moment in time.

He slid her bra straps down her shoulders and paid homage to her breasts, licking each crowning peak as if he'd been bestowed a treasure. She felt the restraint in his big body.

He skimmed her hip with his hand, touching her through the thin material. She arched her hips, seeking, wanting more.

It was a little awkward, though not uncomfortable as he finished taking off her bra and panties, but then she was gloriously naked beneath the sky and his gaze.

Juliette got the impression Sven felt awkward when he reached into his jeans and pulled out a condom. Far from awkward or embarrassed, she appreciated his forethought. Once she'd tested clean and thanked the powers that be, she'd vowed never to have unprotected sex again. She reached into the slitted pocket of her dress and pulled out her own condom to show him. He smiled as she tossed it aside. She was eager, suddenly impatient to have him inside her.

Condom-sheathed, he hesitated. "Tell me if I'm going too fast," he said, "or you're uncomfortable or…"

She reached for him, opening her legs, inviting him, urging him. "Sven, just…please…"

He nudged between her thighs and she gasped as he entered her. It had been a long time. She was tight and he was large, but bit by bit he nudged and she stretched, welcoming him.

He rested inside her, giving both of them time to

adjust to one another. And then he started a slow, long, in-and-almost-out rhythm. He shifted, pulling her legs around his waist, moving faster, driving harder, taking her higher and higher until it felt as if she were soaring, carried by the joining of his body with hers, the celebration of flesh against flesh, spirit with spirit until she lost herself somewhere in the blue sky and the orgasm that rocked through her as she'd never been rocked before.

9

JULIETTE STRETCHED, surprisingly unselfconscious in her nakedness given how prickly she could be at other times.

"Are you warm enough?" Sven asked. The breeze blowing in off the lake had grown stronger.

"I'm just right. That was stupendously good." She reached over and lightly touched his hair.

He didn't have to ask if he'd satisfied her because it was written all over her face, but it was good to hear "stupendously good" nonetheless.

"I concur. I am a very happy guy right now." He caught her hand up in his and pressed a kiss to her wrist. He felt a sense of freedom, hedonism, here on the blanket with her, soaking up the sun. "It's nice lying in the sun naked. I can't say that I've ever done this before, but I like it. It could be habit form-ing." Damn, he was talking to a woman with an addiction. What a stupid thing to say. He pushed up on one elbow. "Juliette, I didn't think... I mean... crap...talk about ruining a moment with my foot in my mouth."

She turned her head on the sheet, looking at him, laughing. "Sven, it's okay. I'm actually flattered you think naked sex with me in the sun could be habit forming. At least I think you meant with me."

He wouldn't want to be here with anyone else. He traced the bottom line of her breast with his fingertip. "Of course I meant you."

"I told you I'm an alcoholic. The last thing I want is for people to tiptoe around me or act all freaked out about it. That's one reason I just keep quiet."

He wrapped on arm around her and pulled her to him, fitting her against him. "Okay, then. I'm not going to tiptoe around it or you. Tell me about it. I've done some research online."

She looked surprised. "You looked it up?"

"Yeah. Why wouldn't I? I wanted to know and I realized I didn't have any facts. So, I know about alcoholism, the disease, the treatments, but I don't know your story."

She stroked her fingers over his forearm, which was resting against her belly, not looking at him. "My parents are both alcoholics." A portion of his heart sank, his mother's concerns still fresh in his mind. They were alcoholics and so was she. Hereditary. "My mother's a crying drunk and my dad's a mean drunk who likes to throw things and hit people." She smoothed her thumb against his skin. "I learned early to make myself scarce." She paused and looked him dead in the eye. "I started drinking when I was fourteen. I just didn't get it. All I knew was that I hated my life and when I drank, I got to be someone else. I didn't cry like my mom and I didn't raise Cain like my dad, so I didn't think I had a problem."

He *hurt* inside for her. "You got any brothers or sisters?"

"Nope. Just me."

"Your folks are still alive, right?"

"Oh, yeah. I got in touch with them a couple of times when I was going through my twelve steps." He knew about the 12-step program at Alcoholics Anonymous from his research. "All I can tell you is you can't save someone else if they don't want to be saved. And even then, they have to do it themselves."

"You still in touch with them?"

"No. I can't deal with their alcoholism and they can't deal with my sobriety. The only thing a drunk hates more than himself is a sober drunk. I think it's that whole lowest-common-denominator thing."

"You lie down with dogs, expect to get up with fleas?"

"That's close. And it sounds as if you're not in danger of catching any fleas in clan Sorenson. Merrilee was telling me about your mom being so excited about her granddaughter."

He was almost embarrassed to admit it in light of her family history. "Yeah, my folks are great. They have their moments, but overall, they're very tolerant. My sister-in-law, Darnita, is African-American and she was pretty nervous about how my folks would feel about the race thing, but Mom and Pops have loved her from day one."

And he had to admit he resented the hell out of his mother's attitude about Juliette's disease. Nor had Marge been too damn happy about Juliette being married twice. But once they met, once his mom had actually seen her and talked to her, everything would be okay.

"That's good. I'm sure it just works better when everyone gets along."

"You'll meet them. Mom and Pops that is. They're coming to the play."

"Merrilee mentioned that."

The very fact that she was so non-committal spoke volumes. Most women would be telling him how much they were looking forward to meeting his parents. But then again, Juliette wasn't most women and that was for dead-ass certain.

"So," he said. "Tell me about flying, about why you love the sky so much." Every instinct inside him said it was all linked to her childhood.

"What? We sleep together once and you feel like you can ask me twenty questions?"

"Something like that. And just think. This is only question number two...well, maybe three. And you were just about to tell me about flying."

She sighed. "You don't give up do you?"

He was discovering a newfound determination he'd never needed before. "Not on the things that are important to me."

A pause stretched between them as his words settled in the space, the wind rustling the grass around them. He'd just told her she was important to him. Finally, she spoke.

"When I was really little I'd leave the house and climb the tree in our yard to get away. I'd sit up there in the leaves and hide. That worked for a while, but then my folks figured out where to find me. I'd always think, if I could just be a little farther up, up there in the sky, they couldn't find me. They couldn't get to me up there."

He hoped he never met her dad...or her mom. He could just see her as a kid, scared, crying, being dragged out of her tree. It made him want to hurt someone or break something.

He tightened his arm around her. She wrapped her hand about his arm and he felt as if she was taking solace in him. He hoped she was. "Then one day old man Haddrick who lived next to us went into the crop-dusting business. He busted me one day after a month of me sneaking into the cockpit of his plane. But he was nice about it. Instead of sending me home, he took me up and it was a done deal. I loved flying and the sky. It was as wonderful, even more than I'd dreamed it would be. After that, old man Haddrick would take me up with him every time he had a job. My folks never figured it out."

"Is that when you knew you wanted to fly?"

"No. I was just a kid who knew she liked being up in the sky. Then old man Haddrick had a stroke. His daughter moved him in with her, sold his plane and that was that."

"Damn."

"I felt bad for him, but to tell you the truth, I felt worse for me."

Her level of honesty surprised him. It must've shown on his face.

She shrugged. "I was a kid used to looking out for myself. I wasn't real empathetic. I dropped out of high school and got married to get out of the house. I figured out pretty early on that was a mistake and at least went back and got my GED and then I got a divorce. It never occurred to me I could actually fly the plane, so I decided I wanted the next best thing and got a flight attendant job. I married again in the middle there and figured out that was a big mistake, too. Derrick and I met in a bar and we only got along when we were both drinking. The problem was we both had to sober up somewhat every day to go to work. He was an airline mechanic. We split. A friend once asked me if I thought we'd have stayed married if we'd both gotten sober. Heck, no, we'd have never gotten married if we'd both been sober long enough."

She slid her finger down his chest. "And that's a pretty frightening bedtime story, isn't it?"

"I don't frighten easily."

"Apparently not."

He hated the shadows that appeared in her eyes when she talked about her past. He was sorry he asked. Not that he couldn't handle it, but he didn't want her to have to go through it all over again.

And he knew exactly how to dissipate those shadows. "Not to change the subject, but to change the subject..."

That earned him the smile he'd hoped for. "Yes?"

"I see that you came prepared, as well." He nodded to the cellophane-wrapped condom she'd tossed aside earlier.

"I did."

"Well, I believe a perfectly good condom is a terrible thing to waste and yours has an expiration date on it."

"It does? I don't know how I missed that."

"I have no idea, but it's clearly set to expire in an hour."

"Really?"

"Honest to Pete."

"Well, what do you think we should do about that?"

"I think—" he dragged his lips over her breast to capture her nipple in his mouth and sucked until she gasped and he released her "—you should..." He caught her waist in his hands and rolled to his back, pulling her on top of him. Her legs naturally braced on either side of him. "Climb on top and let me enjoy the view."

Juliette leaned forward, sliding her already-wet sex along his bare thigh. She kissed the column of his neck, nipping little kisses that darted through him like desire-laden arrows that went straight to his dick. Her breasts rubbed against his chest, her nipples teasing him, taunting him to touch them, play with them, make love to them. He caught them between his forefingers and thumbs. Her low, soft moan vibrated against his skin.

When he couldn't stand it anymore, when the need to be inside her was more than he could take, he rolled on the condom. A wicked little smile playing about her lips, she eased down onto him...and then back up. Again and again and again until he thought he would lose his mind with the need to feel her silk channel all the way around him.

"Juliette...baby...please..."

"Patience."

Just when he thought he had her rhythm, she

plunged down, taking him all the way inside her. "Ahhhh."

Head thrown back, bracing her hands on his thighs, she ground down and around on him. But it wasn't until he felt her muscles tighten around him, squeezing him and her body convulse with pleasure that he allowed himself the ecstasy of coming…and coming…and coming.

JULIETTE WALKED BESIDE Sven, her hand in his. He was a touchy-feely kind of guy and she was finding that she liked it quite a bit. She was finding that she liked everything about him more than quite a bit. She'd decided to open herself up to experiences, but it was all happening at light speed. Adopting Baby, taking their relationship—whatever it was, and she was more than happy to leave it undefined—to the next stage.

The sun had sunk below the horizon on their way back, a waxing moon rising but still low and heavy in the sky. It had to be approaching 11:00 p.m. They'd spent about nine hours together…and she'd enjoyed every minute of it.

"I had a lovely date with you, Sven Sorenson."

"So did I." He brushed his fingertips against her temple. "It doesn't have to end now. You don't have to go."

She was tempted, ever so tempted. But she needed time to think, to digest and process. She needed time to orient herself around all that had happened today. Her and him. Baby.

"I need to go home." As much as she'd enjoyed herself and his company, she really needed to be in her own space and alone.

"I understand."

She wanted to make sure he did. "It's not—"

"I know." He laughed. "It's not personal." He put his hands in his pockets and simply looked at her and she realized it had been kind of an inane thing to say. Before, the first time she'd said it to him, it hadn't been personal. But now...

"Okay, well, I guess there's no way it's not personal at this point, huh?"

He nodded. "That's pretty much the way I see it."

Juliette hesitated and then closed the space between them. She wrapped her arms around Sven's waist and felt a rush of relief when he put his arms around her in return. She leaned into him, resting her cheek against his chest. His heartbeat thumped strong and steady beneath her face. She wanted to make sure he understood. She didn't want to hurt him, so if that meant leaving herself a little vulnerable, so be it. "Sven, it's not because I haven't had a good time. I've had such a good time. I'm not sure when I've ever enjoyed myself so much." If it sounded silly to him, then it sounded silly to him but she decided to just throw it out there. "I want to lie in my bed and savor it. I just want to hug the day to me and go back through it. Does that make any sense?"

"Yeah. Yeah, it does. I guess I'll lie in my bed and savor it, too." He yawned. "Or I might go to sleep. Woman, I'm tired. You wore me out."

"Ha. Blame it on me. You wore yourself out." She plunged forward. Now that she was talking, she couldn't seem to shut up. "And I need to think...well, about everything."

"I'm not so sure I get that. Sometimes people overthink. Sometimes you just have to *be* and go with the flow."

Surrender. Serenity. Accepting the things you couldn't change, having the courage to change the things you could and the wisdom of knowing the difference. It was the flow and intellectually it made sense, but sometimes it was hard to walk that path. And she still needed her space tonight.

"I hear you. Sometimes it's hard to do that."

"When you're flying, you adjust your stuff to the wind currents, don't you?"

"Of course."

"So, take what you do up there and apply it down here. Life on the ground can be the same as it is in the air if you let it."

She tucked that away to digest. She'd try to wrap her head around the notion. "Okay, I'll think about it." She stood on her tiptoes and pressed a kiss to his cheek. "Good night, then."

Instead of releasing her, he tightened his arms about her. "Tomorrow?"

"God willing and the creek doesn't rise, it will arrive." He brought out a playfulness in her.

"You've spent too much time around Merrilee."

"My third-grade teacher used to say it all the time."

"Okay, Ms. Smarty-Pants, so assuming tomorrow comes, what do you have going on?"

"I'm working on a couple of wind chimes."

"Would you like some company?"

Would she? She'd never had anyone else around when she was working on the chimes. She kind of got into a zone, but there was a part of her that wanted to see him again. There was a part of her that knew something this good between them couldn't sustain itself, so she needed to enjoy every minute of it while it lasted. "I'm used to a certain amount of alone time, but if you wanted to bring your sketch pad that might work."

"I said company, not conversation." He grinned. "I don't talk all the time."

He actually had a good energy. He was fun, but he wasn't manic. He could be playful, but he was also peaceful. "Okay."

"Are you going to feed me breakfast?"

She laughed at his temerity. "You're pushing it, Sorenson."

"You don't make it easy for a man, Miller. We'll

make it a joint venture. How about I bring sausage and jelly and you're in charge of the eggs, toast and coffee."

"You'll have to do the toast, too. I'm out of bread."

"You drive a hard bargain but okay. Deal. How about ten?"

She liked her Sunday mornings. She always rose early, did a little yoga routine and then spent a couple of hours online scanning the *New York Times* and the *Anchorage Daily News. That* she wasn't willing to give up. Ten would be cutting it close. "Ten-thirty."

"You drive a hard bargain."

"Consider yourself lucky you're coming."

"Now, *that* sounds like a promise."

She was still laughing when he kissed her. The man never ceased to amaze her.

10

JULIETTE LOOKED AROUND her house with a different eye now that it was about to be seen by someone else. And it wasn't as if it was just anyone. It was Sven and she found it a little scary—okay, a lot scary—how much it mattered to her what he thought of her place.

She'd decorated in shades of yellows, blues and whites. Sheers fluttered in the breeze, blowing through the open windows, carrying the wind-chime songs inside. The sun cut a swath of light across the yellow-and-white-gingham sofa. In the corner, a small fan oscillated on low. She didn't need to cool the room. She simply liked the movement of air.

She'd lived alone since her second divorce. She didn't entertain. She didn't invite people over. Merrilee had dropped by a couple of times, but for the most part her space was her own. And now Sven would be a part of her space.

She was nervous. In fact, if she had his phone number she'd call and cancel. Unfortunately, she didn't, so she was stuck.

She smoothed her hand over the front of her dress. She was *not* wearing this for him. Of course, she wore pants when she flew and most of the time when she was in town, but at home it was always a dress. They were less restrictive than shorts or pants. Even in the winter, she'd crank the heat so she could wear a dress. From the time the temperatures hit above freezing, she was all about going barefoot. She liked the feel of the cool wood floor and the textured pile of the rugs beneath her feet.

The distinct rumble of a diesel engine sounded in the distance. Her heart began to thump against her ribs. Why was she so jumpy? The man had seen her naked. They'd been intimate twice in broad daylight underneath the Alaskan sky. Why was she such a case now?

Because, where she lived, her private space was even more intimate than sharing her body, that's why.

She busied herself turning on the coffeepot she'd prepped earlier. She liked her coffee strong and dark. Sven was out of luck if he didn't.

He pulled up outside and slammed his door. Her heart hammering in her chest, she crossed to the front door and opened it and then the porch door as he was climbing the stairs.

Her heart leaped at the sight of him. His hair was a shade darker than normal and she suspected it was still wet from his shower. A T-shirt from an annual salmon derby hugged his shoulders and chest, while worn jeans rode low on his hips. It was the same thing she'd seen a hundred, make that a thousand, other men wear back in North Carolina and here in Alaska, but on him it was flat-out sexy. And now that she knew what treats were underneath those jeans and T—good grief, she was turned on just *looking* at him.

She realized, with a start, that it was the first time she'd ever seen him in anything other than boots. He wore a pair of dark brown leather sandals.

"Good morning," she said.

"Morning."

He sounded almost as nervous as she felt, which must have been some auditory misperception on her part because she couldn't fathom this gorgeous, self-assured man with a case of the jitters.

"Come on in." She stepped aside and he came into her house.

"These are for you. There were kind of limited choices in the flower department."

All her angst dissipated. It was a little strange, but there was a rightness about him being here in her den. And the flowers were beautiful. She'd been so busy eyeing him like a hungry cat with a salmon steak that she'd totally missed the flowers in his hand.

"Thank you. I love fireweed. You couldn't have made a better choice even if you had other options." She felt as if her insides were smiling at the gesture. She regularly picked a bouquet of wildflowers when they were in season, but it was a different feeling altogether when someone else brought them for you. "Let me put them in water."

She took them and went into the kitchen to find a vase. Sven followed her, looking around in interest, a bag in his hand.

"Nice place," he said, nodding. "Bright and sunny. I like your colors."

It was the part of herself she kept tucked away, shielded from the rest of the world. She basked in his words and the appreciative look on his face.

"Thanks, I like it." She filled a glass pitcher with water and added the flowers. They were beautiful right there next to the sink.

He placed the bag on the counter and pulled out the items. "Sausage, bread and jelly, ma'am."

She could barely think, sharing the tight space in the kitchen with him. It was as if he filled all her senses, as if an energy hummed between them, fine-tuning her body.

"So," she said, "are you starving?" *Because I'm*

hungry for you right now. "The coffee is—" she looked over at the pot "—just about ready."

He locked his laser-blue gaze on her and the look in his eyes relayed a message similar to the one filtering through her brain. "In a minute." He took a step toward her and she could swear she felt the heat pulsing off him. She licked her suddenly dry lips. "First, I'm going to tell you hello properly." Another step closer—God, yes—and he bracketed his hands on either side of her, trapping her between the counter and his big body. She liked being trapped…by him. His glance slid down her. "I like the dress."

She felt tight with anticipation. "Just so you know—"

"Yes?"

"I would've worn a dress anyway this morning, even if you weren't coming over. I like to wear them at home." She might want him, but she needed him to know she didn't dress to please him. She dressed to please herself.

"Message received. I still like it."

Good, they were both pleased. If she'd thought her pulse was jumping before… He slid his hands up her arms, his touch fanning the fire already inside her. He cupped her shoulders in his hands and pulled her to him. She loved the feel of his hardness against her softer curves.

She reveled in the taste and feel of him. He

smelled like the sun and wind and he tasted like mint toothpaste.

"Now, that's a proper good-morning," he said.

She linked her arms around his neck, definitely wanting more of the same. "How hungry are you?" she said. It was a rhetorical question. The passion in his kiss and the hard ridge of his arousal against her belly had told her all she needed to know. "I'm thinking breakfast can wait."

"I'm thinking you may be onto something. Do you think we should try a bed this time?"

No. She wanted him right here. Now. "But it's so far away and—"

"I don't need convincing." That was an understatement. His hard-on teased against her. He leaned down farther and canted his head to tease his lips against her neck, just below her ear. His breath gusted across her sensitive flesh as he asked in a low, husky near whisper. "How do you feel about keeping the dress on?"

She was already wet with desire, but his question left her wetter still. "I can't even tell you how much I like that idea—" she rubbed against him and took his hand in hers, bringing his hand to the hem of her dress "—but there's one way for you to find out."

He slid his hand up her thigh to the edge of her panties. She bit her lip, her skin on fire, her breath lodged in her chest. She *ached* for him to touch her. Instead, he teased and taunted with his fingertip, his knuckles brushing against the fabric of her panties until she mewled with need.

Finally, with a soft laugh, he relented and slipped his finger beneath the edge of her undies. He stroked along her labia and her knees threatened to buckle. It was as if a sexual charge had shot through her. He dipped into her wetness. She closed her eyes it felt so intensely delicious to have his finger against her.

"Hmm. You do like the idea."

She reached between them, cupping her hand over the erection straining against the zipper of his jeans. "You seem pretty enthusiastic yourself."

He slid a finger into her wet channel and she gasped. "Uh-huh."

She groaned and dropped her head back. It felt… A second finger joined the first…

"Oh." Anything more was beyond her. He found her clitoris with his thumb and stroked. All coherent thought vanished. It was simply sensation. The ridge of the counter behind her. His heat. His smell. The press of his fingers inside her. His thumb against her magic spot.

She. Was. Coming. Unraveled.

Wave after wave of her orgasm washed through her, over her.

"That was—"

"Just the beginning."

She could barely stand. Her legs didn't want to support her. "You're kidding."

"Do I look like I'm kidding?"

His face was taut with desire, his eyes reflecting the same need she'd just had satisfied. "No, actually, you don't."

"Put your arms around my neck, honey."

She did. Honestly, she wasn't sure that her legs would continue to support her. The next thing she knew, he was picking her up. She didn't offer even a token protest. She liked this sexually intense, serious side of him.

He moved through the den and easily found her bedroom. Shouldering open the door she'd pulled to, he crossed the room and folded back the comforter, placing her on the rumpled sheets. He gentled a hand over her cheek, his gesture tender. "God, you're beautiful."

She was average and ordinary, but when he said it, she believed it. She felt beautiful. His touch and the look in his eyes—she felt cherished, safe. Something she'd never felt with or from anyone before.

She swept her arm along the cotton sheet, not stopping to consider or weigh her words. She spoke from her heart. "Come to my bed, Sven."

SVEN FIXED THE IMAGE in his head, never wanting to forget this moment—Juliette's dark hair contrasting against the white sheets, the curve of her beckoning arm, the softness in her eyes, the languor of her legs draped over one another, the delicate arch of her feet.

He was hers, whether she wanted him or not. She had branded herself on his soul, imprinted in his heart. He slid off his sandals and took off his shirt and jeans, dropping them to the floor. He stretched out on the bed beside her, the sheets cool beneath his heated skin. "I will gladly come to your bed, Juliette Miller."

She kissed him and it was a mix of hunger and passion and something that hadn't been in her kiss before. There was a giving, a reaching out, an opening up.

Still clad in her white sundress, she moved over him and began to explore him with her hands, her fingertips, her lips and tongue. She licked and kissed down his neck, over his chest, her tongue dragging arousingly over one nipple and then the other. She moved across the plane of his belly, nipping at him, creating the most incredible sensations over his skin.

She tugged his briefs down his hips, looking up his body at him, a question in her eyes. It was as if they were communicating on a level outside of words. He knew what she was asking. He nodded.

"I'm fine. I was checked on my last physical and there hasn't been anyone since then."

She didn't touch him with her hands, but she dragged her warm wet tongue up the length of his shaft and rimmed his head. Done. If she did that one more time it would all be over…and he wasn't ready for it to end. That wasn't the way he wanted her this time.

He reached down and dragged her up his body. "I'm going to take you."

Her eyes glittered with hot desire. "I want you to take me."

He didn't have to tell her, she seemed to know. He donned a condom. She rose, pulling her dress up and off. She tossed it aside. Her panties and bra followed. Silently, she turned her back to him.

He moved into place behind her, the need to possess her, to make her his a raging need inside him. He felt a fierceness as primal as the ritual they were about to embark on that all animals had been doing since time immemorial. He leaned forward and kissed her neck and then lightly bit it.

Juliette gasped, her head thrown back, back arched. She bent over, lowering her shoulders to the mattress, thrusting her buttocks back, opening herself to him.

Her sex glistened, beckoning him. Clasping her hips in his hands, he entered her. She rocked back on him, taking him deeper. She met each of his thrusts with her own, plunging back on him. It was hard and fast. An alpha male taking his female. An alpha female, claiming her mate.

She was panting and he could feel her tightening around his cock. As the first cries of her orgasm tore from her throat, he lost the tenuous hold on his self-control and let his own release roll through him. He threw back his head and answered her with his own guttural cry.

As one, still intimately connected, they collapsed onto the mattress. Sven rolled to his side, pulling her with him. His breathing ragged, he lay with his arm wrapped around her, her back pressed to his chest, her legs against his, her buttocks nestled against his groin.

He smiled to himself. *Damn, Alberta.*

He was cuddling. And he liked it.

JULIETTE WINCED SLIGHTLY as she reached up for coffee cups in the cupboard, having used muscles yesterday and then again today that hadn't had a workout in quite some time.

Sven steadied her with a hand on her waist. "Need help?"

"I've got it. Thanks though." She passed him a cup. "Here you go."

"Thanks." He seemed to like touching her. She liked being touched by him. "Want to pass me the other one?"

"Here you are." She handed him another one.

He took the two cups and filled each with dark, fragrant brew. He handed one to Juliette.

"Thanks." God, he was sweet, thoughtful and good in bed—and obviously too good to last. "Cream? Sugar?"

"Straight up." He hoisted his cup.

"It's pretty strong. I don't like weak coffee," she said as she added half a spoon of sugar and hazelnut creamer to hers and stirred.

He sipped. "Perfect. How about a pan for the sausage?"

She passed him a skillet and a spatula. "I made plenty of coffee, so help yourself to refills."

"Thanks, babe."

Juliette didn't know if it was the great sex, the sunny day and breeze sifting through the window and back door, Sven's presence or a combination of all of the above, but she was incredibly relaxed as she cracked eggs while the sausage sizzled on the stove. For all the sexual intensity they'd had together earlier, now things just felt kicked back and at ease between them. It felt amazingly comfortable and right to be moving around in the kitchen, preparing breakfast together.

"Cheese eggs or plain?" she said, speaking over her shoulder to him where he was positioned in front of the stove, a dishrag thrown casually over his left shoulder.

"Either way." He grinned. "I'm not a picky eater."

His grin was infectious. "Let's go for the cheese, then." She picked up the wedge of extra-sharp cheddar she'd pulled out just in case. "And how many pieces of toast?"

"I'll start with two."

He was a big man. She eyed the egg bowl and re-considered. She cracked another two eggs into the bowl. She'd grown used to only cooking for herself.

A couple of minutes later they carried loaded plates out the door to the backyard. Last year she'd fashioned a rudimentary bench from a log, using a hand planer. It had seasoned nicely.

Heaven help her, but her brain seemed to be stuck in sex mode, because she couldn't help thinking if Sven were to lie flat on his back on the log, bracing his feet on the ground and she were poised on top... Another day. Or maybe later today...

They sat next to one another, his arm brushing against her elbow and just that contact sent a charge through her. The man had quite the effect on her.

"I eat out here most of the time when it's warm enough. It's not the views at Shadow Lake, but it's not bad, huh?"

The cabin sat on top of a rise offering a vista of trees, sky and mountains.

"Very nice. Good eggs."

"Thanks." She didn't know if it was the sex that had worked up such an appetite on her part or if it was simply sharing a meal on her backyard log, but it was delicious. She bit into her buttered toast spread with a thick layer of the jelly Sven had brought over. Yummy! "The salmonberry jelly is amazing," she said as soon as she finished chewing and swallowing.

"My mom makes it every year and sends some home with me. I think this is the best batch yet."

She couldn't compare since she'd never tasted the other, but it was kick-butt tasty. "I was so green when I moved to Alaska, the first time someone mentioned salmonberry jelly I thought it was something to do with the fish." She pointed with her fork toward the salmon printed on the front of his T-shirt.

Sven laughed. "Are you for real?"

"For real."

"Maybe you shouldn't tell anyone else that," he said, teasing her.

"I know." She glanced around at the clearing. "Do you think I need to put up a fence for Baby?"

"I don't think Baby's going to have to be fenced at all. I think it's more likely that she's going to be under your feet all the time. She looked pretty attached already. I think Baby's going to want to be wherever you are."

They finished up breakfast and silently he rose, holding out his hand for her plate. She handed it over. "Thanks."

She was so unused to someone doing things like that for her, but she could so easily get used to it, to him. She shrugged off the notion, disquieted by the thought. There was no point in getting used to any of it.

They were in this for the short term. One day at a time.

Her head heard her loud and clear. She just wasn't sure that her heart was getting the warning message.

11

THAT EVENING SVEN SAT at his desk reviewing the budget sheets for his next job. This was the part of his business he hated, but he was buzzing on such a cloud from the day spent with Juliette, he figured he might as well get the crappy stuff out of the way.

He glanced at the charcoal sketch he'd propped against his desk lamp. It was from yesterday, when she'd been napping after their picnic. He thought he'd done a pretty good job of capturing her air of guarded vulnerability.

His cell phone rang. His mom. They hadn't spoken since they'd talked about Juliette several nights ago. That wasn't unusual—their conversations were sporadic—but he knew she hadn't been a happy camper when they hung up.

"Hi, Mom. How's it going?"

He listened with half an ear as his mother gave

him a blow-by-blow of Pops's indigestion and a case of gout that was interfering with his running schedule. He closed the schedule book and leaned back, propping his feet on the desk's edge. "I hate to hear that."

"Are you still seeing that woman?"

She tossed it out there, her disdain evident in her *that woman.* Sven sat up, planting his feet flat on the floor. His mother's tone and her words pissed him off.

"That woman has a name," he said, managing a neutrality he wasn't quite feeling.

"Fine. Are you still seeing Julie?"

"Juliette. And, yes, I am." His mom had loved his dog Susie. She'd want to hear about the puppies and perhaps that would smooth her ruffled feathers. "We went and picked out puppies—"

She interrupted him. "This is a mistake, Sven. She has problems. Serious problems."

He forced himself to relax his clenched jaw. "You're not even giving her a chance."

"I'm sure she's perfectly lovely, but, honey, she's an alcoholic and you just can't trust those people not to backslide. You'd be caught up in all that mess and it'd wreck your life. And you've got to think about the kids."

His gut knotted. There was a reasonableness in her argument he simply didn't want to hear. He rubbed his hand over his face. "Mind your own business, Mom."

"I am minding my business." Her voice escalated in pitch and volume. "You're my son and that makes you my business. Any kids you have are my grand-kids, so that makes their mother my business."

Sven pushed to his feet and paced across the room, opening the front door to look out on the lake. "Let's talk about putting the cart before the horse, Marge."

"Pops and I always taught you and your brother that you shouldn't—"

He finished for her. "Date a girl you wouldn't marry because you never know who you might fall in love with." How many times had they heard that?

"That's right. You were listening. And I'm telling you this Juliette is a mistake."

"Too late, Mom. The die's cast."

Her gasp echoed on the other end. "You mean she's pregnant?"

The level to which his mother could incorrectly fill in a blank was mind-boggling. "No, she's not pregnant." The idea, however, did give him a kind of warm fuzzy feeling that would just further freak Marge out.

"Then what do you mean, 'the die's cast'?"

"I mean I love her." It felt strange, but good, to say the words aloud.

"No." She practically wailed the denial.

"Yes. Yes, I do."

"But, honey, of all the women in the world to choose from… What about that nice girl from Palmer you were seeing last year?"

"Mom, you could at least give her a chance." Exasperated, frustrated, he ran his hand through his hair. "I've never known you to be like this."

"Neither of my children ever dated a woman who was not only an alcoholic but had two failed marriages before, either."

He was fairly laid-back. He'd always been slow to anger, but his mom was definitely pushing the edge of his envelope. "You're treading on thin ice."

"I'm telling you I don't approve and I think it's a mistake."

"I want you to like her because she's a good person and because she's important to me." He paused and drew a deep breath. "But ultimately, it doesn't matter whether you approve or not."

A deathly quiet filled the line. Finally she spoke. "I see."

It was impossible to miss the tears clogging her voice. His mother sometimes cried over greeting-card commercials, but she'd never cried because he'd wounded her. It was painful to him that he'd hurt her, that hadn't been his intent, but he wouldn't have her speak about Juliette that way and it wasn't fair of Marge to dismiss Juliette, to prejudge her.

"Mom—"

"You've been seeing her how long? Not even a week, but you're already in love? And you'd put her before your family? You'd choose her over us?"

Sven chose his words carefully. Once something was said, it couldn't be unsaid. A man, or woman, could apologize all day long, but once spoken, words couldn't be taken back.

He hadn't told Juliette how he felt because she was skittish and he wanted to give her time, but there was a connection there, if she'd only let it grow. But the bottom line was, loving her wasn't contingent on her returning his feelings. "I shouldn't have to choose one over the other, Mom. You always told us parents might not like their children's choices, but parental love was unconditional. This is the way it is. I love her, which means I'll defend her and champion her because that's my code."

"Maybe Pops and I shouldn't come up for the play."

He rubbed at the back of his neck, stress knotting the muscle. He would not be dictated to by his mother. Did she really think if she threatened to boycott the play he'd opt to not see Juliette again? "That's totally up to you. I love you and Pops and I'd love to see you. I think you'll enjoy the production. You and Pops are important to me and Juliette's important to me. I'd like for you guys to meet, but only if you can meet her with an open mind and respect

for who she is. That said, if you decide not to come,
I understand."

The tension on the line could be cut with the proverbial knife. "And that's the way it is?" she said.

"That's the way it is."

"Okay."

"I love you, Mom."

"I love you, too, son."

He didn't have a good feeling in his gut.

MONDAY MORNING JULIETTE walked into the airstrip
office. It was a glorious day. She'd slept better last
night than she had in a long time. Well, make that
ever. She'd fallen asleep with Sven's scent on her
pillow.

Merrilee looked up from her seemingly endless
stack of paperwork. Juliette supposed that's what
running an airstrip, a bed-and-breakfast, a small
town and keeping her husband's books for his hardware company would do for a woman. Lots and lots
of paperwork.

Juliette smiled at both Merrilee and Alberta, who
was pouring a cup of joe. Juliette wondered just how
many pots Merrilee brewed in a day. A lot.

"I hear you have a new puppy," Merrilee said,
beaming at Juliette.

Juliette nodded, heading for the coffee—and the
muffins. She'd overslept and was starving. "Well,

she's not home yet, I have to get in my supplies first, but she is *sooo* cute."

"You'll have to bring her in so we can see her."

"Oh, yeah. Wait until you see the flight jacket I ordered for her."

Merrilee chuckled. "I can't wait."

"I hear you have a new boyfriend," Alberta said, her smile knowing.

There was a time, in the not-too-distant past—as in the middle of last week—when Juliette would've simply stonewalled the matchmaking psychic Gypsy. And for a second her armor slipped into place…and then she shrugged it off. She was going to live and take what life was handing her and quit being afraid it would all evaporate around her like a good dream interrupted by the alarm clock.

"It sort of seems that way."

"Well, do tell." Alberta looked pleased as she peeled the paper off the bottom of a muffin, as if she was personally responsible for Juliette's new-boyfriend status. Whatever.

"I don't know that there's really much to tell." Except that Sven was wonderful. "We've done a little hiking, went on a picnic, went puppy shopping and just sort of hung out." *And had rock-my-world sex.* "He's good company." *A great kisser and an even better lover.*

"You're good for him," Alberta said around a mouthful of muffin.

Juliette blinked, surprised by Alberta's pronouncement. "I am? In what way?"

"You've made him stretch himself and find out what he's made of. Or at least he will."

She couldn't help herself. She had to ask. "You really think I'm good for him?"

"I do. He's happy with you."

Her words thrilled Juliette, but she was leery of being too happy. She hedged it. "Well, I didn't notice him being exactly depressed before."

Alberta laughed. "Sven's discovering his depth with you. He's growing. It's a really good thing. Like I said, you're good for him."

Merrilee spoke up. "For what it's worth, I agree with Alberta. You are good for him."

Juliette's heart felt as if it was soaring within her chest. It was as if everything she'd ever wanted, things she hadn't even dared to admit she wanted, were hers. She, Juliette Miller, brought something special to beautiful Sven Sorenson who had led a charmed life. It was really almost too much for a woman to take in.

"That's good. That makes me happy." She didn't recall ever feeling this way, not even when she flew. She loved flying, but this was different. This was... well, something incredibly special and she wasn't even up in the air.

"Then I'd say we've got ourselves a win-win situation," Alberta mused. "You're happy. He's happy."

Yes. Yes, she was. She had known peace and a contentment that came with her sobriety. She had learned to love herself and find joy in herself, but this…this was so far beyond any of that. This was what Sue had meant when she said Juliette could be sober or she could be sober and live. This was living…and it was joyous.

Merrilee's phone rang on her desk. "Excuse me, ladies." She picked it up. "Good Riddance Air and Bed-and-Breakfast. Oh, hey, Marge. How are you?"

Alberta said in an undertone, "That's Sven's mother."

Merrilee's smile faded as she listened, the voice on the other end strident, upset. "Sure.… Okay.… No problem." Marge Sorenson obviously had plenty to say on the other end of the line, and Juliette wasn't trying to eavesdrop, but Marge was obviously agitated and quite loud and Juliette clearly heard Marge mention Juliette's name. Merrilee, in the meantime, looked increasingly uncomfortable.

She interrupted Marge. "Look, let me call you back in a bit. I was in the middle of something… No, it's okay. I'll call you back. Yeah. In a while."

She hung up the phone and reached for her pencil. "Okay, so did you have any questions or conflicts with today's schedule?"

"I'm not sure because I still have to look it over, don't I?" Merrilee was so jangled she didn't remember that she and Juliette hadn't gone over the schedule yet. This was really weird. Juliette couldn't just walk away and wonder all day. It would drive her nuts.

"I do, however, have a question about that phone call," Juliette continued. "You know I don't usually stick my nose in any other people's business and I've always kept to myself, but I couldn't help hearing my name. And Mrs. Sorenson was very obviously not happy."

Juliette felt slightly nauseated, apprehension forming a ball in the pit of her stomach.

Merrilee shrugged as if it wasn't a big deal. "Marge was calling to cancel her and Edgar's seats for the play."

"I see." And she did see. It didn't take a rocket scientist to figure it out if Marge had said Juliette's name. "And they're canceling because Sven is involved with me."

Merrilee looked absolutely miserable. "You'll have to talk to him about it, Juliette."

Alberta rubbed her arm consolingly. "Ebb and flow, sweetie, ebb and flow."

She wanted to burst into tears. Sven, this really great man that she was so in love with that she couldn't see straight because if she could see straight—she would've never allowed herself to believe that this could all work out—had this superperfect family that had always gotten along beautifully, but now that she was involved chaos was erupting. She'd known from the first time she'd ever heard about them that she wouldn't fit in. Heck, she hadn't even met them and it was already a mess.

"Talk to him first, Juliette," Alberta said.

"Hon, I can see it all over your face that you're upset," Merrilee said. "And I don't blame you. I'll call Dalton. He can cover for you today and you go find Sven and get this sorted out."

What the hell was it with her? Her childhood had been disastrous, her marriages, too. She'd finally found some measure of calm, but then she got involved with Sven and once again madness came along. Obviously she did best in a solo, isolated state of being. She stood tall. She was a big girl. She'd had a fun couple of days and now it was back to life as usual. The alarm clock had gone off and the dream was over. "Dalton had the weekend."

Merrilee waved a dismissing hand. "You know Dalton, he won't mind."

Juliette pulled herself together, cloaking herself in the mantle she'd so foolishly discarded for a period of time. "I'm fine. I'm a professional. I'll do my job. I'll talk to Sven later."

And that would actually work out better because she was fairly certain if she tried to talk to Sven right now, she'd burst into tears and then she'd really feel somewhere beyond foolish. That was if she even did talk to him. Perhaps it was best to make a swift, clean break. What was there to talk about? She was a problem between him and his family. Eliminate her from the equation and there was no problem.

All the old feelings of inadequacy swept through her, over her. She felt in the bottom of the pit she'd been in for so long—hopeless, helpless, no way out. The equally familiar craving to dull those emotions, to take the edge off, the temporary relief of anesthetization, washed over her, as well. What difference would one, or two or more drinks make?

SVEN WANTED TO PUT HIS fist through a wall. Merrilee had filled him in on the morning's events. He'd been waiting all day for a chance to talk with Juliette. However, she'd neatly avoided him all evening.

She'd shown up late for rehearsal, kept herself surrounded with other people, and now she'd managed to leave without him being able to catch a moment alone with her.

If, however, she thought for one minute that he'd just let it go, she was in for a rude awakening. They were going to talk about this. She wasn't going to shut down and shut him out.

He knew where she lived. He got into his truck and was so intent he nearly missed her Land Rover parked on the back side of Gus's. He pulled into the parking lot. Fine. He could show up at Gus's, as well. And if she still wanted to ignore him, the place closed at ten. She had to go home eventually.

He walked into the bar and the room grew quiet,

except for the jukebox playing "Are You Lonesome Tonight?" Great choice. And for the first time he resented living in a town where everyone knew everyone's business.

Doubtless by now everyone knew his mother had canceled on the dinner theater because she disapproved of Juliette. Now Juliette was avoiding him like the damn plague and he couldn't remember ever being this angry with his mother.

That disappeared the instant he spotted her. Juliette was sitting at the bar, raising a glass with a pale pink liquid that looked a whole lot like a cosmopolitan in a highball glass with a slice of lime on the rim. His heart lodged in his throat.

No! No! No!

He didn't realize he'd spoken, actually shouted the words, until Juliette startled. She swiveled on her seat to face him.

"What are you doing?" Sven said. "You don't want to do that."

She eyed him with a mixture of consternation and coolness. "I assure you I do." She deliberately took a swallow.

If she didn't have enough sense... He wasn't going to just stand here and watch her do something so self-destructive. He never thought he'd have to protect her from herself, but he'd take on whomever he had to. He crossed the room in three long strides.

"Put it down right now, Juliette."

"You do not tell me what to do or when to do it. Do I make myself clear?"

"Goddammit, I love you enough—"

"You can stop right there. It's seltzer, you know, sparkling water, with a splash of cranberry juice. It's light and refreshing and my drink of choice these days." She looked around the room, her face tight, her eyes guarded. "And for those of you who haven't heard, you'll figure it out soon enough after this little display. I'm Juliette…and I'm an alcoholic. A recovering alcoholic, but an alcoholic nonetheless. Once an alkie always an alkie." She looked back at Sven.

"And I'm not sure what it is you love me enough for, maybe to disagree with your mother over seeing me, but it's not enough to trust me. I don't need a keeper. I am responsible for me." Each word rang out like a shot. She put a five-dollar bill on the bar, her hands unsteady, rose to her feet and walked to the door, head held high, back ramrod straight, and strode out into the May evening.

He started to follow. Alberta—he hadn't even noticed her in the room, his attention had been so focused on Juliette—stayed him with a hand to his arm. "Leave her be, Sven. She just got a big dose of humiliation and heartbreak. She needs some time alone."

His gut was so damn twisted he couldn't think straight. He'd just made a big-ass mess of everything. "How much time?"

Alberta shook her head, her eyes worried. "I don't know."

Sven received several sympathetic looks. However, Curl walked by and gave him a look similar to the one Juliette had sent his way.

"That was just wrong," the taxidermist said. "I've been where she is and it's not an easy path. She has to make her own choices. That was just wrong."

Sven had never landed so knee deep in shit as now. He dropped onto the stool Juliette had vacated.

"I'll take a Jack and Coke. Actually, just make it a Jack."

MERRILEE SLIPPED THROUGH the swinging door between Gus's and the airstrip office. Bull followed her.

"Are you about to do what I think you're about to do?" he said.

"Alberta's the psychic, so I can't answer that precisely. I can, however, tell you what's about to transpire. I'm going to pull Juliette's application and I'm going to call her emergency contact, Sue Dickens, because in my book this qualifies as an emergency. That girl is hurting and hurting bad. I'd go out to her place, but she's not going to talk to me because she knows I'm friends with Marge. Trust is already a big issue for her and she's not going to trust me with her heart breaking right now. And it is breaking. She needs someone and I'm going to see that she gets someone." She planted her hands on her hips in defiance, daring him to tell her to mind her own business. "Now what?"

"Now I think that's a good idea."

"You do?" Bull sometimes accused her of interfering when she shouldn't.

"I do. You're burning daylight. Get on the horn with this Sue."

While Merrilee was pulling the paperwork, Bull asked, "Just for curiosity's sake, would it have made any difference if I thought calling her was a bad idea?"

Merrilee retrieved the sheet of paper and smiled at her husband. "No. It wouldn't have."

He returned her smile with a satisfied nod. "That's what I thought."

12

JULIETTE HELD HERSELF together until she got through her front door…and then she fell apart. Gut-deep sobs tore through her as she collapsed onto the sofa.

She pounded her fist on the cushion. She…hated…him.

She had been okay. She had been content with what her life was. She had known what her life was. And then…she hated him so much she could barely breathe… He had shown her a glimpse of paradise, had made her want more, dream, hope. She had thought she could have what the rest of the world had—someone who understood her, who got her—

Her cell phone rang, startling her out of her internal rant. Sue—it was her ringtone.

"Hello."

"I'm sorry, sweetie."

"How did you…" She finished on a hiccup.

"Mrs. Swenson called. She is so worried about you. She thought you needed someone, but she didn't think you'd see her…or anyone else. She said if it was ever an emergency, this was it."

Juliette pulled herself up off the couch and went in search of toilet paper in the bathroom. "Why does everyone suddenly think I need a keeper? I've been looking after myself just fine my whole damn life."

"I'm not telling you how you should or shouldn't feel." Sue was as pragmatic and matter-of-fact as she always was. "I'm not telling you that Sven was right or wrong in what he did and how he handled that situation tonight."

"Hold on a minute. I need to blow my nose."

"Okay."

Juliette put the phone on mute and set it down on the sink. Sue didn't need to hear her. A few seconds later she picked it back up, clicking the mute off. "I'm back."

"Look, I know you and I know it was embarrassing—"

Juliette interrupted. Angry all over again. "It was so humiliating. I wanted the floor to swallow me whole."

"Yeah, well, that only happens in science-fiction movies. But I know it had to be bad."

She marched across the room and yanked open the freezer door. "And then he stands there and announces that he loves me like that. That was actually worse than him blabbing that I'm an alcoholic, because the truth is I am an alcoholic." She grabbed the bag of chocolate chips out of the freezer. "I hate him."

It was a lie and she knew it was a lie, but she hurt inside and she wished she could hate him. She popped a couple of chocolate chips in her mouth, letting them melt against her tongue. Chocolate might not help, but it sure couldn't hurt.

"Hmm, so the truth is you're an alcoholic but it couldn't be the truth that he loves you?"

How could he? Didn't he know she'd simply wreak havoc on his life? She hadn't even met his parents yet and already she was upsetting their perfect apple cart.

"I don't know him," Sue said. "Never laid eyes on him, but your boss seems to think a lot of him."

"Yeah? Well, Merrilee and his mother are good friends, so that's not surprising."

"I don't know. I've got some friends that I love dearly and I think their kids stink, but that's just me. Anyway, she seems to think almost as much of him as she thinks of you."

Juliette poured herself a glass of water and didn't comment. She'd try to hold her peace while Sue had her say. The chocolate did help.

"But the man cares about you…and she cares about you…and that's not being your keeper, that's just…well, caring about you. Obviously he's got some things to figure out. I think alcoholism is pretty new to him and from what Mrs. Swenson says—" it took Juliette a second to realize Sue was talking about Merrilee, she just didn't think of her as Mrs. Swenson "—being in love is brand-new to him, too. And he's three for three in the newbie department, because so is making a fool of himself in front of the whole town and being at odds with his family. And he might've gone about it in heavy-handed jackass kind of way, which sounds like it's not normally his style, but the man loves you and he panicked. I can't tell you how to feel or what to think, but you might want to cut him a little slack."

Juliette rubbed the glass of cool water against her forehead. "I have to think…"

"I know. Do you need me to come? Mrs. Swenson says she can send a plane to pick me up. In fact, that was what she was pushing for. I told her to let us talk first."

Merrilee was going to send Dalton to pick Sue up for Juliette? It blew her away that Merrilee might care that much, that anyone other than Sue would care that much. And then there was the fact that Sven was at odds with his parents over her. And now everyone in town would look at her differently because she was a drunk and she'd caused a rift in the venerated Sorenson family. Her head was spinning and she didn't want to think about any of it right now. She'd had enough drama to last her the rest of her life. She appreciated Sue, but she didn't need the additional drama of her arrival. Juliette just wanted to be unconscious for a while.

"I just want to get some sleep."

"Are you okay?"

Juliette knew Sue was asking if she was okay not to have a drink. As much as she just wanted to have it all go away, to numb it all, block it all, having a drink wasn't an option. As she knew all too well, all the crap would still be there tomorrow and she'd just feel bad about the alcohol. No drink. She'd face her problems head-on; feel her pain head-on without the temporary anesthetization of alcohol that really only intensified the madness. For whatever she was and wherever she was right now, she would maintain her sobriety and her sanity.

"Yes, I'm fine. I'm just tired. It's been a long day. I promise I'll call if I need to." *The best time to make the call was before you took that first drink.*

"Okay. I do have one question for you before you go." Sue paused. "Why did you go to the bar?"

The question took Juliette by surprise. "Gus's is the only—"

"I know about Gus's." Merrilee, no doubt. "But you *sat* at the bar. Why?"

"I was drinking seltzer and cranberry juice." She knew she sounded defensive. She *felt* defensive. She hadn't compromised her sobriety with alcohol.

"That's what Mrs. Swenson said, but you sat at the *bar*. Is that something you normally do?"

"Well...no."

"But you sat there knowing that sooner or later Sven was going to show up, probably sooner rather than later. So, why'd you park yourself on that bar stool?"

She didn't know. She just had. "I don't know."

"That might be something important to figure out. Call me if you need me."

THE NEXT DAY, SVEN PARKED his truck by the cabin at Shadow Lake. He'd driven over and checked on his crew and their progress. Things were fine and he'd opted to come back here and work alone on the cabin remodel. That was the beauty of a competent foreman, because right now Sven wasn't fit company for anyone.

He was hammering in some fresh header boards on the cabin's porch when the crunch of tires on gravel and the low hum of an engine heralded company. Whoever it was ought to have enough damn sense to steer clear of him.

Merrilee's dusty Jeep Cherokee pulled up next to his truck. Alberta rode shotgun. He ran a weary hand over his head. He knew he'd fucked up. He hadn't slept worth a damn last night. And while he loved both these ladies, he really wasn't in the mood to hear anything, be it advice or indictments. That was the very reason he'd had his cell phone off all morning. He didn't want to talk to anyone except Juliette…and she wasn't talking. He should know. He'd called her three times, each call going to voice mail.

Hammer in hand, he met them just as they got out of Merrilee's truck, hoping to head them off at the pass. "I'm kind of busy—"

They kept coming, both their faces set in an expression of sympathetic dread. The hair on the back of his neck prickled.

Merrilee interrupted. "Sven, I've got some news. Your mom couldn't get in touch with you. Your dad's alive but it's touchy. Edgar had a heart attack."

The hammer slipped through his fingers and thudded to the ground. No…

"He was at the hospital in Palmer, but they're on their way to Anchorage with him because he needs bypass surgery."

"How's Mom?"

"Falling apart. Eric and Darnita are with her, but…" But he and his mom had always been close. She must be frantic about Pops. Sven couldn't— wouldn't—even think about Pops not making it. He had to pull through. And Sven had to get to his family.

"You got a plane on the runway waiting on me?"

"Yes. Dalton."

He didn't want Dalton. "Where's Juliette?"

"She's on her way back from Bear Creek."

"Does she know?"

"She does."

If something happened to Pops… "I need her."

He didn't realize he'd spoken the words aloud until Merrilee answered him.

"I know. I know you do, honey."

He looked at Alberta. If ever he wanted to know the future… "Is he going to be okay?"

Alberta shook her head regretfully. "I don't know, Sven. I just don't know. I'm not getting a reading on it."

He picked up the hammer, already unhooking the carabiner with his truck keys from his belt loop. "Let's go."

JULIETTE CUT STRAIGHT to the chase when she walked into the airstrip office. The flight back from Bear Creek seemed to have lasted a lifetime.

"How is he?"

Weariness and worry bracketed Merrilee's mouth. "Edgar or Sven?"

"Both." Juliette clasped her hands together to keep them from shaking. Sven must be beside himself. Recrimination and self-loathing surged through her. She had brought this on him and his family.

"Edgar's about to go into surgery. It's touch-and-go. Sven's en route." She looked at Juliette and said quite simply, "He needs you."

There was a starkness there that tore at Juliette's soul. And Sven was strong. She'd seen it in him, recognized it in him the day he'd picked Bruiser. "He has his family."

"But they're not you. They're not his mate. He loves you, you know. All of you."

"I love him, too, but…"

"If you leave him to face this alone—"

Juliette interrupted. "He won't forgive me. I know."

Merrilee shook her head. "Oh, no. He'll forgive you, but will you forgive you? You're the one who has to live with your decisions."

Merrilee didn't understand. Juliette had Sven's best interests at heart. "I wreak havoc, I bring chaos. It's always been this way. When I keep to myself, it's as if it's contained, but look what happened. He met me and boom, chaos. He was at odds with his parents when this happened—because of me. What if his dad doesn't make it?"

"It's called life, Juliette. And, if you'll pardon me for saying this, it isn't always about you. Life gives us tests and obstacles. It's what forges character and makes us stronger people and better human beings if we rise to the challenge. We can't grow without pain." She pulled off her glasses and cleaned them on the hem of her shirt. "You love him?"

"Yes. Enough to take myself out of his path." She realized in that instant—that was why she'd sat at the bar last night. She'd wanted to drive him away. If he wouldn't walk away from her, she'd do him the favor of pushing him away.

Merrilee put her glasses back on. "That's not your call. We're each responsible for ourselves. He's a grown man, respect and trust him enough to let him make his own decisions."

Juliette knew what she knew, regardless of what Merrilee said. "I'm going to run this soap over to Jenna's spa." Her run to Bear Creek had been to drop off a group of fishermen and pick up a carton of the wild-rose soap that Jenna was stocking. "I'll fuel up for the Kodiak run when I get back."

Merrilee shook her head. "Dalton's covering Kodiak. He's refueling out of Anchorage and picking it up." She shrugged. "It was efficient and made sense. The rest of the day is yours."

"But—" It did make sense that Dalton would pick up that trip from Anchorage, but she'd counted on working. She needed to be up there in the sky.

"You're fine, Juliette. Maybe Jenna can work you in at the spa, or maybe you've got a wind-chime project going or you just want to sit outside and soak up some of this beautiful May sun. The rest of the day is at your disposal. Seize the moment."

Juliette stood there, locked motionless in indecision. It was one thing to hide behind the obligations of her job, but how could she possibly sit out in the sun or placidly craft a wind chime or any of the other options while Sven waited anxiously for his father to pull through surgery or not? How could she? The bottom line was...she couldn't.

She'd felt her whole life as if she'd never had anyone to count on, so she'd insulated herself. The past couple of years she'd been safe and sober, but she'd also been stuck in a holding pattern. It was time to soar, it was time to give. For the first time she truly understood that in moving beyond the fear, in giving—truly, the sky was the limit.

She cleared her throat and Merrilee looked up as if she hadn't known that Juliette had been rooted in that same spot. "When I finish this delivery," Juliette said, "would you clear me for Anchorage?"

Merrilee smiled. "Bull could use something to do." She nodded to the crate of soap on the hand truck. "He can handle the delivery. You're already cleared for Anchorage...and Sue's on standby to pick you up at the airport and get you to the hospital."

"You were that sure of me?"

"Hopeful, honey, hopeful. I know a strong woman when I see one."

Tears rushed to the back of Juliette's eyes. That was probably one of the nicest things another woman had ever said to her. Impulsively she reached out and hugged Merrilee. It felt good.

A family like Sven's, a family like she'd never had, needed to be protected at all costs. She'd never meant to harm them, to bring trouble to their door.

She was strong enough to go and set things to right. She'd be strong enough for both of them.

SVEN STOOD AT THE waiting-room window overlooking the sprawl that had become Anchorage. An antiseptic smell permeated the air. A television mounted high in the corner was tuned in to some daytime talk-show host. At least the volume was set to low. On one side of the waiting room, his grandmothers flanked his mother. They sat huddled, talking in undertones.

Darnita and Eric sat in the corner opposite the television. Eric had his arm around his wife's shoulders as she napped with her head against his chest. Sven didn't think his brother was asleep, but his eyes were closed.

Sven stood, alone, simply waiting, cold, despite the sun slanting through the tempered glass. Down the hallway, Pops was fighting for his life. It all held a surreal note. It was as if his world had suddenly capsized on him, as if all the anchors that had kept him grounded were disappearing.

He didn't want to think about the grim possibility of his dad not making it through, of Pops not being there for his wife, his sons, his grandchildren. Sven pushed those thoughts aside. In the distance, the sun glinted off a plane. Was it coming or going? It really didn't matter.

He thought about Juliette. About the scent of her

hair as he lay in her bed, her head tucked in the crook of his shoulder, the laughter in her eyes when they were picking out the puppies, the slide of her naked body over his, her sharing the stove space with him, scrambling eggs while he cooked the sausage.

He realized the low murmur of female voices had ceased. He sensed her, smelled her, recognized her footfall across the tile floor, before she even touched him.

Wordlessly, Juliette joined him at the window and slipped her hand into his. Her hand, small but strong and warm, wrapped around his. In that one gesture she offered solace and strength. In that moment, it was as if a weight had been shifted, a burden shared.

He looked down at her. "Thank you for coming."

She nodded, her brown eyes dark with concern and inquiry. "Are you okay?"

He squeezed his fingers around hers. "I'm fine." *Now that you're here.*

"Any news?"

He shook his head. "For now, no news is good news. It should be about another half hour."

"Do you need anything?"

He smiled at her, his heart immeasurably lighter. "Not now."

However, there was a look in her eyes that gave him pause. "I'm glad you're okay. I needed to know you were."

He spoke from his heart. "I needed you here."

"Sven, I don't want to bring any drama to this, but I can't stand that your involvement with me has come between you and your family. I wanted to make sure you were okay, but tell your mom I'm bowing out."

She was worth fighting for. Even if she was the one he had to fight. "No."

"Your family…what you all have…it's something special, precious."

"So is what we have." There was no bluff, no bravado behind his words. He spoke with conviction. "And it's not as if I can't have both my family and you."

"Sven, your dad had a heart attack."

"Obviously."

"So, I get involved in your life and your family disapproves and your dad winds up in the E.R. I'm not good for you. I'm not going to bring this to your family. I'll just go back to being alone—"

"No."

"But—"

"No. You are not going to go back to being alone. My father had a heart attack because he needed bypass surgery and didn't know it. And it wasn't a family argument that brought this on. He was training for a marathon, plain and simple."

"Oh."

"Oh is right. You, us, none of it had anything to do with Pops having a heart attack."

"But your mom called and canceled, obviously upset—"

"Yep. And then Pops today. Two totally unrelated events. So, try as hard as you can, you can't blame yourself for Pops's heart attack. And try as hard as you might, you're not going to get rid of me so easily. I'm in for the long haul."

13

JULIETTE STOOD STOCK-STILL, letting his words go through her, sink into her. *I'm in for the long haul.*

They felt more sincere than the marriage vows mouthed by either of her former husbands.

She nodded slowly. "Okay." It was an acknowledgment not an affirmation. She needed process time and they were standing in a hospital waiting room.

A short woman with short blond hair and Sven's brilliant blue eyes crossed the room. Juliette vaguely recognized her. It dropped into place for Juliette. She had seen the woman in passing during Chrismoose the first year Juliette had worked in Good Riddance. Sven's mom. Apprehension clutched in her gut. It was hard to meet someone when you knew they already disliked you. But Sven had needed her. And this woman's husband and mate was fighting for his life on an operating-room table, so how she felt about Juliette didn't matter at the moment. This wasn't about Juliette.

"Mom, Juliette Miller. Juliette, my mother."

It was strange. Sven didn't move into a different position, but it was as if he grew bigger than he already was. It was as if he positioned himself between her and his mother, as if to say anyone would have to go through him first to get to Juliette and that wasn't going to happen. It was subtle and unspoken, but it felt like the grandest gesture ever.

"Mrs. Sorenson. I'm so sorry about your husband." She held out her hand as she nodded in the direction of the hallway, which was about as close as she came to knowing where the O.R. was.

The older woman shook her hand, looking from her to Sven to their clasped hands and nodded slowly. "Thank you. Thank you for coming for my son."

"I had to," Juliette said simply and quietly.

Marge Sorenson held her gaze, her look searching. Juliette opened her heart, letting Marge see inside her, letting her see how much Sven had come to mean to her.

"I see."

And Juliette knew she did.

Sven looked from his mother to Juliette, a faint frown furrowing his brow, obviously perplexed by their nearly silent exchange. It was one of those estrogen moments when a man just didn't get the different plane that women could operate on.

Juliette indicated the shopping bag she'd carried in and set on the floor. "I picked up some chicken and a couple of side dishes. I didn't know if anyone had had a chance to eat. It's easy to forget to take care of yourself. Plus, that's what we do where I'm from."

For the first time ever she acknowledged her past, her roots, without regret or rancor. She was what she was, the good, the bad and the in-between all mixed up into one person. She was sure, however, the scales tipped in the direction of the good. Standing here, talking to this woman, she no longer felt like the one in the white T-shirt club with the grease stain.

"I'm kind of lost," he said. "Something's going on but I'm not sure what."

His mother smiled and patted his arm. "That's okay, son. I just realized something important. Everything in life comes with risk. This was a good risk because you're a different man. I should have trusted you and your instincts." She looked back at Juliette. "Merrilee said you were precious and she's right. And I know now why my son loves you."

Juliette's heart, already full, overflowed. There was no longer room for indecision or inadequacy in her life.

"Thank you. That means a lot." Juliette looked at

Sven, knowing full well her heart was in her eyes. "And I love him, too."

It didn't feel strange or awkward to say the words out loud. It simply felt good and right. Love was meant to be shared, not clutched close in fear. It left you vulnerable, but she also understood, standing here now, just how strong it made you as well, to love and give love.

His family looked on, somewhat bemused. Much as everyone had last night at Gus's when he'd declared himself.

"For real?" he said, a slow smile curving his mouth.

"For real."

His mother offered a nod of satisfaction. "Of course you do, otherwise you wouldn't have walked through that door."

And in the middle of what was one of the happiest moments of her life, the surgeon, his mask pushed up to his forehead, walked in.

Sven heard the shower shut off in the hotel bathroom. Pops was doing great—as great as a man could be doing after going through open-heart surgery. The doc had been pretty sure that he'd be moving to a regular room tomorrow.

He'd been so relieved he'd damn near cried. And he was glad Juliette was staying over in Anchorage tonight with him. Yeah, he had his family around, but he'd wanted her to stay.

The bathroom door opened and she stepped out from a cloud of steam. Her short dark hair clung damply to her scalp. She'd wrapped a thick white towel around her sarongwise, which left the creamy slope of her shoulders and legs bare. He would never tire of looking at this woman.

He shifted on the king-size bed, patting the spot next to him in invitation.

She stood for a moment, simply looking at him. "Lord, you are beautiful, both inside and out."

For her to say that to him... Because this woman had seen into his soul, into the depths of him and thought he was enough, meant the world to him. That in finding her, he'd found an important part of himself—a strength and fortitude he'd always been unsure of. "So are you, honey, so are you. Come here."

"But my hair is wet, so it'll get you wet."

"Come here." He held up his arm and she laughed as she climbed up on the bed and settled next to him in the crook. He rubbed his fingers against the curve of her shoulders, loving the play of smooth skin beneath his fingertips. "Mmm, you smell good, fresh."

She turned her head to inhale against his arm. "I love the way you smell."

"Really? How do I smell?"

She shrugged against him and smiled. "I don't know. It's just your scent. You."

She wrapped her fingers around his arm. "I didn't expect that today...you know, with your mother."

"I knew if she met you she'd like you. I was wrong."

Juliette stiffened next to him. "I thought she did like me."

He supposed he shouldn't tease her. "My mother adores you," Sven said.

"It was the chicken," she said with a smile. He liked it when she made little jokes.

"That didn't hurt. Seriously, it was you. I just want to say thank-you all over again."

"I'm really glad your dad is okay."

"You and me both." He tightened his arm around her. Today had certainly taught him not to take the people he loved for granted. "Mom's in her element now, hovering around him."

"They're obviously devoted to one another."

"Yeah, they are." The same way he would be devoted to her, now that he'd found her.

"And your brother and his wife are very nice."

"Wait until you meet that kid of theirs. She's something else." He wanted her to know he was planning forward. "They all liked you. I knew they would—not that it would've mattered if they didn't." Not that he particularly wanted to bring it up, but they needed to clear the air and he might as well get it out of the way. "I owe you a big apology. I don't know what I was thinking. I just walked in at Gus's and it wasn't that I didn't trust you, but I was so damn scared when I saw you sitting there at the bar." And that was an understatement.

She rolled onto her side, wrapping her arm around his middle. "No. I'm the one who owes you an apology. I think on some level I set that up. It wasn't a conscious thought, but when I look back on it…well, I knew I'd caused a rift between you and your family. I knew the reason had to be the alcoholism, so if…I don't know…I guess I set you up to freak out and you did and then I wanted to be indignant, so I own that."

"How about we were both wrong and let's just let it go?"

"That works for me," she said.

Her towel had fallen open a bit, offering a distracting view of thigh and hip. He traced his fingertip over the curve of her hip and felt her tremble against him. "I need to adequately thank you…but I want to hear you say something to me again. Now that it's just the two of us with no distractions."

Juliette teased her toe along his leg, a gleam in her eyes. "I'm really excited about getting a dog."

He cupped her hip in his palm. "Try again, babe."

"The set for the play is coming along nicely."

"Uh-huh." He smoothed his thumb along her hip bone.

"Your family is nice." And her breathing wasn't quite even.

"Juliette…"

Her eyes growing serious, she reached up and smoothed her hand over his face, her fingertips feathering against his brow. "I love you. I love you in a way I never thought I could love anyone."

Those were perhaps the sweetest words he'd ever heard spoken, coming from her. "How do you feel about kids?"

She laughed.

What was so damn funny? "I'm serious."

She peered at him. "You are serious. I don't know, Sven. I'm thinking, given my family history, it's best if I pass on that. Can't we just take it one day at a time?"

Now that he knew what he wanted, had found what he wanted, he wanted it all—no more sliding by, no more settling. "I don't see why we can't talk about a future. I love you and you love me. I'm not looking for anyone else. I don't want anyone else. I think we should get married. And Alberta predicted this."

"What? Alberta predicted what?"

Oh, hell. He'd figured she'd known, that somehow it had gotten back to her the way everything did in Good Riddance. Well, she was about to find out now. "You and me. When she rolled back into town, she told me I was ready for love and I told her she was nuts. Then she told me you were the one and I told her she was really nuts."

"Really? Really?" Uh, her voice escalated on that second really. "And what was so wrong with me?"

"Because I'd always liked my women simple and uncomplicated, and, babe, we both know there's not a thing uncomplicated about you."

She relaxed somewhat against him. "Somehow that feels like a backhanded compliment. So, is that why you asked me out to your place for dinner? Because of some prognostication from Alberta? And now you want to talk about getting married because she predicted it? That's crazy."

"It would be…if it was the case. I asked you to dinner because I was intrigued by you."

She was somewhat mollified. "That's good, I suppose."

"And I asked you to marry me because I love you. Alberta has nothing to do with it. And I do think you'd make a good mom."

She tensed against him once again, but if they were going to make a go of it, they had to be able to talk to one another.

"How could you possibly have any idea what kind of mom I'd make?"

"I saw you with Baby."

"Baby's a dog. There's a big difference between a dog and a kid."

"Okay. But haven't you had any of that biological-clock-ticking business going on since you're thirty-two already?"

She looked at him as if he'd taken a stupid pill. "Amazingly enough, given my advanced age, I haven't experienced that particular phenomenon."

"That was the wrong thing for me to say, huh?"

"Ya think?"

He slid his hand over her hip to one plump butt cheek. "Can we still fool around?"

"I don't know. I might need a nap...given how old I am and with my clock running out of time."

While he squeezed the rounded fullness beneath his palm, he nuzzled at her neck. "No problem. I don't mind at all when you nap first."

She drew in an unsteady breath and rolled, putting her crotch in direct contact with his, and rocked against him. *Oh, yeah.*

"Or I suppose I can nap afterward."

"Are you saying I put you to sleep?"

She laughed—he loved to hear her laugh. "Never. You simply relax me with great sex so that I can sleep afterward."

He grinned as he peeled the towel back, leaving her naked. "Great, huh?"

"Ah, I see you just want your ego stroked."

"Actually, I was hoping to have some other things stroked, as well. If we have to limit it, I'll forgo my ego if you'll..."

"Needy."

"Admittedly." He caught her nipple between his thumb and forefinger. "I need this..." He bent his head and teased his tongue over the pebbled point. "And this…"

"Me, too," she murmured as he showed her just how much he loved her.

A FEW WEEKS LATER, JULIETTE met Sue, whom Dalton had flown in, at the door. The community center had definitely been transformed. Tables had been draped with white cloth and a buffet table, provided by Gus's, stood against the far wall.

"I'm so glad you came." Sue was family as far as Juliette was concerned, in a way she'd never felt about her own folks.

"Hey, a night out at a dinner theater and the chance to see you—I wouldn't pass that up."

Juliette grinned. "It's not quite what a lot of dinner theaters are where waitstaff serve meals on trays, but it works here. We go with our own flow here in Good Riddance." She took Sue by the arm. "So, come on and you can meet everyone and leave your purse at the table while you go through the buffet line."

Sven's folks were seated at a table with Merrilee and Bull. The doctor had cleared Pops—as she'd been instructed to call him—for travel, and this was their first outing since his surgery. The empty chair at the table was Sue's. Juliette made the introductions.

"It's nice to put a face with a voice and a name," Merrilee said.

Edgar grinned. "We saved you a seat. This is the rehab table."

Marge glared at him.

"What? Oh, damn. I meant because I've got a new heart valve, and Gimpy over there—" he waved toward Bull "—has a broken arm. I didn't mean…"

Both Juliette and Sue laughed. Juliette patted him on the shoulder. "It's fine, Pops. We know what you mean. And Sven comes by it honestly, that's for sure."

Marge sniffed. "All of our sons' bad traits come from him and his side of the family."

"Speak of the devil…"

Sven slipped from behind the curtain and headed for them. "Sorry about that," he said when he got to the table. "The tower kept collapsing." Flashing one of his most charming smiles, he offered his hand. "You must be Sue. I'm Sven. It's a pleasure to meet you."

"Oh. My," Sue said.

"It's okay," Juliette said. Even Sue's pragmatism was no match for Sven Sorenson's charm. "He has that effect on women."

Sue shook her head. "You never stood a chance, did you?"

Sven grinned and put his arm around Juliette's shoulders. "She put up a damn good fight, didn't you, babe?" He murmured for her ears only, "And she's still fighting, but I'm going to win yet."

There they were back to that same circling on the marriage topic.

Juliette merely shook her head. "Okay, I've got to get backstage, but I hope you enjoy the production. And let's all hope the tower doesn't fall."

Sven feigned a dark look. "She's power mad."

Everyone laughed. She was mad—mad about him.

Halfway through the production it hit her. She'd come so far and now she needed to take that final leap of faith. And she knew as surely as she knew her own name that it was time. She'd never been more certain of anything than her and Sven and their future.

Finally, the entire cast and crew took to the stage for the closing bow amidst a standing ovation. Good Riddance was an appreciative crowd to play to.

Tessa Sisnukett, the director, thanked everyone for coming and another round of clapping ensued. Juliette spoke up at the tail end of the applause. She wanted to catch everyone before they started leaving—and before her courage failed her.

Public speaking was so not her thing, but a woman who'd finally learned to fly and soar and feel safe without ever leaving the ground had to do what she had to do.

"While everyone's still here...and if everyone will

stay on the stage…tonight we're going to do some improvisation." Murmurs rippled through the audience. "Sven and I have been having our own play and I kept flubbing my lines—" she turned to him "—but if you want to give it another try, I think I finally got it right."

"This is the one we've been rehearsing?"

"Uh-huh."

"Okay, then. Juliette, Juliette, you are my star in the east…wait, sun in the east."

She could feel his happiness radiating off him. She felt pretty giddy herself. Good Riddance was seeing a new side of her, the side she'd kept hidden, the side she'd never acknowledged even to herself. "Wrong play, Sven. Wrong lines."

"Oh, damn." He looked out at the audience, "See, this is why she and I were backstage with the set design."

Everyone laughed. There were a couple hoots and claps from the rear.

Sven cleared his throat. "Juliette Miller, everyone here knows I love you." That earned him a few catcalls. "Most of them were in Gus's that night and those who weren't heard about it before the next morning, considering the way news travels here."

That garnered several more laughs.

"I think the next line is yours," he said, giving her a sweeping bow.

"Sven Sorenson, I love you. I love you the way I never thought I could love anyone."

A collective sigh rolled through the audience.

He looked her in the eye. "You sure you've got the next part down correctly? Do you trust me?"

She nodded and he continued. "Everyone pretty much knows we got puppies from the same litter..."

What the...? "I think you've got a totally new script."

"Work with me."

"I trust you," she said. And she did, with her heart and her soul.

"So, I think it's a shame to keep those puppies apart. I think puppies are much happier with both a mom and a dad around." He dropped to one knee. "Will you do me the honor of being the mother of my puppy?"

Marge stood up. "Sven Sorenson, that is the worst line, improvisational or not. I taught you better than that."

Edgar tugged on her. "Sit down, Marge."

Marge grudgingly resumed her seat, but kept talking. "Well, it's just bad writing. What? She's going to want to tell our grandchildren that their father asked her to be the mother of his puppy? Dear God."

Edgar patted Marge on the arm and looked up at the stage. "Son, you know how women are. They take this stuff seriously. You might want to try again."

"Juliette, I love you. Will you marry me?"

"I will."

The words had barely passed her lips when Edgar yelled out, "The ring. The ring."

Juliette looked at Sven, totally befuddled. "The ring? What ring?"

"Damn. Redo." He reached in his blue-jeans pocket and pulled out a box. "Juliette, will you marry me?"

She looked dumbfounded at the jeweler's box in his palm. "You had a ring... How... Huh?"

"I was going to propose tonight, right here, anyway. You just beat me to it. But it's all worked out. And trust me, I was a whole lot happier knowing you'd finally got your lines right."

"But what if I'd said no?"

"Then I'd have kept asking until I wore you down."

"Hey, you gonna kiss her or what? 'Cause if you need a stand-in, I can help out." Juliette wasn't sure who it was that yelled but she didn't really care.

"I think I'd better kiss her, 'cause the other option isn't going to work out well for any of us."

And he did, earning them another standing ovation.

Epilogue

"I LOVE IT HERE," Juliette said as they settled on the blanket in the picnic spot she'd come to think of as theirs, the place where they'd first made love.

She settled her head against Sven's belly. They probably looked like a human T to the hawk flying overhead, with her lying perpendicular to him. In the clearing next to them Baby tackled her brother and the two puppies rolled around, play growling, only to leap to their feet and chase one another again. "They like it, too. And Bruiser's always so good with her. Even though he's twice as big as she is, he never hurts her."

"That's because she's little and quiet at first, but she's feisty inside, just like you."

He ran his hand through her hair and she sighed aloud in contentment. She held her left hand up, letting the sun catch the facets of the diamond on her finger that bespoke the promise between them. This man would stand beside her, with her, in front of her, if need be, to take on the world. And she'd do the same for him.

And she knew him well enough to know something was on his mind. It had been for a week or more. She hadn't pressed him. When he was ready he'd throw it on the table between them. That's the way it worked with them.

"This would be a fine spot for a house, don't you think?"

She'd thought the same thing the last time they were out here. "Honestly, I've always thought it would be a better choice than where Dalton and Skye put theirs, but to each his own."

"Yep, nice and private, as we know. Great views of the lake, the mountains, the sky."

"I know. From the front porch you'd see all that." She swept her arm out in front of her. "And that view's not too shabby, either."

She'd been waiting for what she felt was the right time to talk to Sven about where they were going to live once he finished his jobs in Good Riddance. She knew he'd always been something of a rolling stone and if that was important to him, then she'd figure out a way to make it work—they'd figure out a way to make it work. As a bush pilot, she could find work in other areas, but she'd started thinking more and more that maybe the two of them together would make pretty decent parents.

Bruiser zoomed past with Baby in hot puppy pursuit.

Sven laughed. "The dogs like it, too."

He put the sketchbook he always brought with him on the blanket to the right of her and flipped over a couple of pages. "What do you think about that house?"

She had the sense it wasn't a casual question. Her heart began to thump harder in her chest. "It's beautiful but not intrusive."

"Yep. And what do you think of this?"

He flipped another couple of pages. A typed document was there between the sketch paper. It took her a second to realize what she was looking at.

She sat up and turned on her knees to face him. "You mean…?"

That slow smile that she loved so much lit his eyes and curved his lips. "Yep."

"This land is yours? You bought it from Dalton?"

"Dalton agreed to sell me a parcel and he thinks we'd make good neighbors, but it's not mine. It's ours. Look again. Both of our names are on the property."

There it was, both of their names. The two of them together.

Just when she thought it couldn't get any better it did. She'd never known how high she could fly with her feet still on the ground.

* * * * *